MW00613380

"If I show you my library card, can we get to know each other better?" Boyd asked with a roguish smile.

Mia pulled herself up haughtily. "Sir! I'll have you know that librarians don't make deals."

He grinned. "I hear librarians do it between the covers," he said huskily.

Old joke or no, Mia threw back her head and laughed.

That did it. He'd held out long enough. He couldn't resist the beauty of her throat, the graceful long curve of it, the creamy softness.

He kissed her on the side of her delectable neck and let his lips linger there. He nibbled a bit, gently yet wild in his hunger for her.

Mia shivered. Her whole body was one heated throb. She was aware of nothing but the warmth radiating from him and the heady male scent that drugged her senses. She could feel the unmistakable need, the hard promise in every line of Boyd's body as he leaned over her, and all she wanted to do was obey the passionate, timeless call of the senses. . . .

WHAT ARE *LOVESWEPT* ROMANCES?

They are stories of true romance and touching emotion. We believe those two very important ingredients are constants in our highly sensual and very believable stories in the *LOVESWEPT* line. Our goal is to give you, the reader, stories of consistently high quality that may sometimes make you laugh, sometimes make you cry, but are always fresh and creative and contain many delightful surprises within their pages.

Most romance fans read an enormous number of books. Those they truly love, they keep. Others may be traded with friends and soon forgotten. We hope that each *LOVESWEPT* romance will be a treasure—a "keeper." We will always try to publish

*LOVE STORIES YOU'LL NEVER FORGET
BY AUTHORS YOU'LL ALWAYS REMEMBER*

The Editors

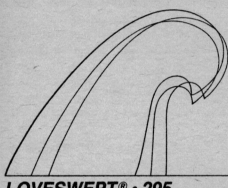

LOVESWEPT® • 295

Margaret Malkind
Late Night Rendezvous

BANTAM BOOKS
TORONTO • NEW YORK • LONDON • SYDNEY • AUCKLAND

LATE NIGHT RENDEZVOUS

A Bantam Book / December 1988

LOVESWEPT® and the wave device are registered
trademarks of Bantam Books, a division of
Bantam Doubleday Dell Publishing Group, Inc.
Registered in U.S. Patent
and Trademark Office and elsewhere.

All rights reserved.
Copyright © 1988 by Margaret Malkind.
Cover art copyright © 1988 by George Tsui.
No part of this book may be reproduced or transmitted
in any form or by any means, electronic or mechanical,
including photocopying, recording, or by any information
storage and retrieval system, without permission in
writing from the publisher.
For information address: Bantam Books.

If you would be interested in receiving protective vinyl
covers for your Loveswept books, please write to this address
for information:

Loveswept
Bantam Books
P.O. Box 985
Hicksville, NY 11802

ISBN 0-553-21947-2

Published simultaneously in the United States and Canada

Bantam Books are published by Bantam Books, a division
of Bantam Doubleday Dell Publishing Group, Inc. Its trademark, consisting of the words "Bantam Books" and the
portrayal of a rooster, is Registered in U.S. Patent and
Trademark Office and in other countries. Marca Registrada.
Bantam Books, 666 Fifth Avenue, New York, New York 10103.

PRINTED IN THE UNITED STATES OF AMERICA

O   0 9 8 7 6 5 4 3 2 1

One

"Don't look now, Mia, but you've got a secret admirer," Frances, the library clerk, whispered. "That man's staring at you."

Mia glanced up from the picture book about dinosaurs she was checking, past the stack of books still in front of her and the freckled-faced boy solemnly watching her, to the man Frances was pointing to.

There was nothing subtle about Frances, Mia thought, nor about the look the man was giving her. If looks could kill, she was one dead librarian.

Oddly enough she wasn't frightened. Six feet and some inches of a lean, muscled body with broad shoulders, a narrow waist, and long athletic-looking legs didn't frighten her. Nor was she intimidated by his thick, chestnut-brown curly hair and aquamarine eyes with spiky dark lashes. Granted, those eyes were a puzzlement at the moment.

Who was this stranger, and why did he have it in for her? She wondered. Had she mutilated his library card? Miscalculated an overdue fine? Forgot ten to reserve the one and only book he had eve wanted to read?

She'd soon find out. He was on his way towar her, and there was no one standing behind th freckled-face little boy.

He placed his hands firmly on the counter an leaned forward so that he was looking directly int her eyes. The gesture was so unexpected, Mia's glanc was drawn momentarily to his hands. They wer large, but the fingers were long and slender and th nails well kept.

Then she raised her gaze to his face. His nose wa narrow and straight; his mouth firm, with a hint o humor at the corners. And he had a Cary Grant clef in his chin that Mia wished for one crazy momen she could run her finger down.

"Yes?" Mia asked in her professional librarian' voice. "Can I help you find something?"

"I don't believe so, Miss Taylor, and as you can see, I don't have any picture books to be stamped."

Mia listened, fascinated. What *was* this guy's problem, and how come he knew her name? she asked herself.

"*May* I have a word with you in private?" the man demanded.

Mia gave Frances the librarian's you-take-over nod and stepped out from behind the counter.

Surprise and admiration flickered in turn over the man's strong, clear-cut features.

What had he expected, Mia thought, amused, a mermaid?

Skirts were short this year, and Mia had nothing to hide. Her legs were slender, shapely, and long for her height, which was exactly five foot five.

"We can talk over here," Mia said, leading the way to one of the San Ramon Community Library's "book nooks."

Mia sat down, glad of the chance to get off her feet. But the stranger remained standing, so Mia had to put her head back to look up at him.

His gaze lingered on the graceful, milk-white curve of her neck. Then he tightened his mouth into a grim line and started off brusquely.

"I'm Boyd Baxter, and I want your mother, the stand-up comic"—he laced the words with contempt —"to leave my father alone."

Mia repressed a giggle but not quite soon enough. His eyes had caught the dimple in her right cheek. His expression softened, then hardened once more.

Mia smiled with gentle amusement. "I'm sorry, Mr. Baxter, but you have the wrong person. My mother's not a stand-up comic but a retired school-teacher and a master point bridge player."

"Please, Miss Taylor," he said, with exaggerated patience. "I wasn't born yesterday. I'll grant you, it's unpleasant to learn that one's sixty-five-year-old mother is a seductress, possibly a gold digger, but the truth must be faced."

Mia flushed with anger. Her eyes smarted with tears of indignation. She was mad enough to kill.

"Don't you dare even suggest my mother is any of those things," she whispered, her voice barely controlled. "I don't know what your game is, mister, but you don't belong in this library. Get out, or I'll call the police and have you thrown out."

One thick, very virile black eyebrow slanted upward. "Suppose I prove it to you?"

"Prove what?" Mia asked. "That my mother is a social security seductress and a gold digger?"

"That your mother performs in the Laff-A-Minute Club, and my dad goes there to watch and cheer her on. After that . . ."

Mia jumped to her feet, forcing Boyd to step backward. Arms akimbo, eyes flashing, nostrils flaring, she challenged him. "After that, what?"

"They go tearing around on a motorcycle Dad bought so he could show your mother he's young enough for her. Dad's seventy. Do you have any idea what could happen to a seventy-year-old man on a motorcycle?"

Mia didn't answer. Pictures were flying through her mind—and they weren't of a septuagenarian on a motorbike.

Mia pictured a thirty-five-year-old man with chestnut-brown hair and eyes the color of Caribbean-blue water bandaged from head to toe, both legs up in traction, and herself in a pink-lady uniform. He would beg to have the afternoon kiddie cartoons turned off, and she wouldn't do it. What's more, she'd switch menus so he got the soft, low-sodium, no-wine-with-dinner diet.

Without warning, those images segued into others. The pink lady had wheeled in a cart of books. Suddenly the bandaged arms encircled the pink uniform. The man pulled the woman close to him, close enough for a kiss. . . . Mia frowned.

Boyd saw her frown. There was very little about this gorgeous librarian he didn't pick up on. Amazing, he thought, how he was tuning in to this person he'd just met.

It was obvious that the pathetic picture of two elderly people risking their lives had gotten to her.

Mia snorted. "Mom's never been on a motorcycle

in her life. She's the original Little Old Lady from Pasadena. She still drives the Chevy Dad gave her fifteen years ago, before he died. As for Mom telling jokes in front of people, forget it. She gets stage fright if anyone in the audience is older than ten. I've seen it happen. You've got the wrong Mrs. Taylor, Mr. Baxter. Somebody else's mother is appearing at this comedy club."

Boyd advanced a step, which put him so close that Mia could feel his warmth and smell his deliciously spicy after-shave. "You wanna bet?" he asked, challenging her.

"Sure, I'll bet. What?"

Your body, Boyd wanted to say. Her skin was truly magnificent, he noticed, like luscious peaches and cream. The curving bell of her ebony pageboy framed broad cheekbones and sweetly shaped lips that curved up happily at the corners. He had a sudden impulse to nibble at those corners, to cup his hands around her derriere in the short tight skirt and pull her to him.

Hey! None of that, he told himself. She was the enemy. Her mother was endangering his dad, Romney Baxter. One of the first rules of war was, don't fraternize with the enemy—or to be more precise, the enemy's daughter.

What should she bet? Mia wondered dreamily. A night on the town? A weekend somewhere?

Oh hell, Boyd thought. Eating wasn't fraternizing. Everyone had to eat. "Loser buys the winner the best dinner in town."

Without thinking, Mia stuck out her hand. "You're on."

It was supposed to be a quick, over-the-net handshake. But the touch of his fingers on her skin sent an unexpected blaze of heat through them both. For one long moment they stood still, staring into each other's eyes, searching for answers.

"I don't want to keep you from your work." Boyd's tone indicated that was exactly what he wanted to do.

What work? Mia thought, dazed by the intense look in his clear, azure eyes and the lingering tingle of warmth where he had touched her.

She watched him bend toward her, noticing the way his head tilted slightly and his gaze focused on her lips.

He was going to kiss her! she realized. Right there in the library!

Boyd straightened up, put off by the look of terror on Mia's face. "I'll pick you up at nine," he said briskly. "Your mother comes on later than that, but you never can tell, she might do her routine early tonight."

Mention of her mother's routines made Mia's temper flare up again. "Wait a minute, I just thought of something. Why don't I have Mom call you when I get home. She can tell you you're mistaken, and that way we won't have to go out together at all."

"Your mother won't be home, Miss Taylor," Boyd said with an exasperating smile. "She'll be at the comedy club with my father."

"Mom!" Mia shouted, letting herself into the house. She had extracted Boyd's phone number from him and wanted her mother to call him that very instant. She would stand within earshot just to hear that arrogant, insulting man eat crow. "Mom!" she called again.

Mia stood stock-still in the entryway. There was no answer. Moreover, the house had an empty nobody's-home feeling.

For a moment Mia was alarmed. Her mother had had a mild heart attack a few years ago. It was the reason Mia lived at home. But, she realized with relief, a neighbor would have called her at the library if there had been an emergency.

Mia struck her forehead with the flat of her hand. Stupid! She had forgotten it was Tuesday, one of her mother's bridge nights.

In corroboration there was the usual note stuck between the sugar bowl and the saltshaker. "There's a casserole in the fridge and a lemon sorbet in the freezer. Enjoy! Love, Mom. P.S. I'll be a little late. You know how the girls love their bridge! Don't wait up."

Mia ate the casserole and had a cup of tea afterward.

She'd won the bet! She could hardly wait to see Boyd Baxter's face when the unknown Mrs. Taylor appeared on the stage and gave Mia a blank stare as she waved wildly.

Maybe, Mia thought, as she took another sip of her tea, she would call out, "Mom!" just to turn the knife a little. After all he had impugned her mother's honor. Then she would smile sweetly at him as Mrs. Taylor said, "Mom who?"

Should she forgive him? Mia debated the answer to that question as she stood before her closet. It was an important decision. What she would wear depended on it.

Recalling Boyd's sea-blue eyes against his tanned, burnished skin, Mia decided on forgiveness. Who wouldn't be worried about an elderly parent staying up late and roaring around on a motorcycle? Boyd's concern showed how much he loved his father.

Mia took a bright fuchsia turtlenecked dress out of her closet and slipped into it. Frowning a little at the mirror, she considered the dress seriously. From the high collar to the black patent leather belt, it was a very smooth, tight fit. In contrast, from the waist to the banded bottom above her knees, it fell in soft, graceful pleats. It was perfect—sexy but in good taste.

But hadn't Boyd been a little more disagreeable than necessary about the situation?

Mia took the dress off and foraged in her closet until she found a white blouse with a Peter Pan collar and a plaid skirt that she had bought when she first started working in the library, on the assumption that librarians dressed sedately.

But suppose he apologized nicely when he realized his mistake and wanted to go somewhere afterward? She thought. She took the turtlenecked dress and patent leather belt out again.

The effect was eminently gratifying. Mia had the satisfaction of seeing Boyd's remarkable blue eyes devour her for a second before his jaw stiffened like a soldier's on parade.

"You look exceptionally lovely, Miss Taylor. I didn't know librarians—"

"Were actually people?" Mia interrupted, amused. "With nice, wholesome mothers and normal instincts?"

"Normal instinct are always to be desired, Miss Taylor," Boyd said. Heaven knew, she was arousing some very normal instincts in him. His heart raced. His breathing quickened. Turn it off, Baxter! he told himself. Now! "So are nice, wholesome mothers," he added.

"Remind me, Mr. Baxter, to dump a bowl of Mom's homemade chicken soup over your arrogant head when this evening's over."

Suddenly he laughed. Mia stared at him, spellbound. His sapphire-blue eyes danced. Tiny laugh wrinkles etched his smooth, tanned skin. His teeth flashed bright and straight between his firm lips.

"You know, Mr. Baxter, you're much nicer when you laugh than when you go around glowering at people." Mia drew her eyebrows together and glared at him.

Boyd laughed again, throwing his head back. "Suppose we declare a truce and call each other by first names. We might even enjoy our evening together."

He put his hand under her elbow and escorted her to his car, a sexy, low-slung Lamborghini.

"It's a beauty," Mia said.

Boyd drew one finger lovingly across the shiny black surface. "It can do two hundred miles an hour."

Mia gave him a sidelong look. "Like father, like son."

"Not exactly. I'm half Dad's age. My bones aren't brittle; my heart's sound; I'm in tip-top condition."

Mia applauded. She leaned over him and pretended to pin something on the lapel of his tan cashmere jacket. "Here's your good health medal."

Mia saw at once it was a mistake. But was it a deliberate mistake? Had she unconsciously intended to get close enough for his arm to snake around her waist and stay there?

"You can't drive a car with one hand!" she protested.

"Sure I can. It's an Italian car. It was made for this sort of thing."

Mia took his hand and placed it back on the leather-covered steering wheel. "I don't want to be involved in an accident before I collect on the best dinner in town."

He darted a glance at her. "Is that the only reason?"

"No. I don't like undue familiarity either."

"Or maybe any familiarity," Boyd murmured.

"Certainly not familiarity with anyone who makes wild accusations about my mother," Mia said indignantly.

"Look, I'm sorry I said that stuff about her being after Dad's money. It isn't true, and I didn't really mean it. I was just hopping mad."

"Inasmuch as we're not talking about *my* mother at all," Mia said icily, "I don't see any reason to continue this conversation."

Boyd shot her a cheerful smile. "Okay with me. Let's change the subject. Have you read any good books lately?"

"Laff-A-Minute looks more like Cry-By-The-Hour," Mia said, as they entered the half-empty, unadorned cellar. "Do they make a living here?"

Boyd shrugged. "Only a few of the comics—mostly the headliners—get paid. The amateurs perform for the experience and the exposure. Customers are obligated to buy two drinks. And the rent is low."

"How do you know?" Mia asked, surprised.

"I hold the lease on the building. I'm in real estate. Lots of it," he added with a cocky self-confidence that seemed more boyish than boastful.

"Oh," Mia said softly. That explained the custom-built Italian car, the cashmere jacket, and the form-fitting silk shirt.

"My Dad got me started," Boyd went on, and Mia could hear the affectionate pride in his voice. "We were in business together until he decided to retire. That's my Dad over there, Romney Baxter."

Boyd nodded toward a man sitting alone at a table in front and to the side of them. From the back Mia could see he had Boyd's long torso, but his neck was thin and frail-looking and his shoulders drooped. Mia had an insight into Boyd's anxiety about his father. But it was somebody else's mother, not hers, he should be concerned about, she told herself.

Romney was watching a young comic perform on stage. Every time the would-be comedian finished a joke, Romney wrote something on a long yellow legal pad.

"What's he doing?" Mia whispered.

"I don't know. Counting laughs maybe."

"He could do that on the fingers of one hand."

The kid up on stage was bombing badly. He tried one more joke. "I saw an old woman changing a flat tire, and I walked right by. Then I thought, what kind of person am I? So I went back and said, 'Have a nice day.'"

The room was so quiet, the guy's breathing was audible through the mike.

"Oh, I feel so sorry for him," Mia said with a little gasp. "How can he stand there and take all that humiliation?"

"Just wait," Boyd said grimly.

Mia's big gray eyes darkened with scorn. "If you're referring to my mother, I assure you, she wouldn't be caught dead in a place like this."

Boyd held up two crossed fingers. "Truce. Remember?"

"You started it," Mia muttered, then returned her attention to the stage. The emcee had reappeared. He smoothly told the young man that his ten minutes on Laff-A-Minute's amateur night were up and thanked him for coming.

"Who knows?" the emcee asked the audience. "Maybe a headliner tomorrow."

Judging from the faint applause, Mia didn't think it seemed likely.

A slim Miss Teenage America-type bounced out onstage next. Her first joke about the torture of having fat thighs drew hoots of disbelief from the audience, and she retreated in tears.

There was some noise behind them, and Mia turned around as a large group entered and was shown to a table right in front of the stage.

"Tourists," Boyd said knowingly.

"How can you tell?"

"The sunburns. They've just come from the East or Midwest and were so thrilled to see sunshine in January, they couldn't stay out of the sun. Californians would be tanned."

Mia groaned. "One of them's a Californian—the elderly woman with the snow-white hair twisted into a bun on top of her head. It's Mary Goudge. She's the most old-fashioned and snobbish of all the members of the library board. She objected to the modern design of the library. She's against all the library's community projects such as the literacy program, because she says it brings a lower-class element into the library. And she's always trying to have books that she personally objects to taken off the shelves. She's completely without a sense of humor."

"If she's so snobbish and humorless, what's she doing at a grungy place like the Laff-A-Minute?"

"The only possible reason is that her out-of-town guests wanted to go to a comedy club."

"Makes sense," Boyd admitted.

Five comedians later Mia said, "This is pretty bad. It's past midnight and no Mrs. Taylor has appeared. Why don't we go?"

Boyd looked at her humorously. "We had a bet. Remember?" Impulsively he took her hand. "Look, we don't have to listen to the performers. Tell me about yourself. Do you like being a librarian?"

"I love it," Mia said enthusiastically, withdrawing her hand.

Boyd took it again and drew one long, lazy finger across her palm. "Tell me what you like about it," he said in a low, sexy tone as he continued to caress her palm.

Everything, Mia thought—The ripples of excitement it sent through her, the touch of his warm skin against hers, the alluring look in those Paul Newman blue eyes of his. Aloud, she answered. "I like books *and* people, and I enjoy serving the community. The best part, though, is the children's story hour. I love to read to the preschoolers and see their eyes widen with interest."

"Have you always been a librarian?"

"Not always. I worked for a public relations firm before I decided to go to college and get a degree in library science."

"So you didn't like P.R. work?" Boyd asked. With her stunning good looks and vivacious personality, Mia seemed more the type to be out in the world dazzling people, he thought.

Mia shrugged. "I guess not."

She certainly wasn't going to tell a virtual stranger the real reason for her career change. A psychologist friend of hers had advised it when Gary Morgan, her fiancé, had left her standing in her wedding gown in the dressing room of the church three years ago, and without a word of explanation, had not shown up for his own wedding.

"Do something radically different with your life," her friend had advised. "Take a long trip, change jobs, find a new sport or hobby. Do anything that will involve you completely and take your mind off what happened."

So she had gone back to school and become a librarian, and it had turned out for the best. Although sometimes she missed the pace of the P.R. firm, on the whole she preferred her work at the library.

Her psychologist friend had been right. The effort involved in qualifying herself for a different career, and then learning a new job, had taken all her energy, so that she had less time to think about Gary. She had begun dating other men, and gradually the wound Gary had made in her spirit and self-esteem healed.

Still, recalling the painful experience of having been jilted caused Mia to tense up. Boyd took her tight little fist and straightened the fingers. For a second her hand lay open and trusting in his. The poignancy of the gesture made Boyd regret having brought her to the comedy club. He leaned forward and started to say, "Let's get out of here," when the emcee called out in his piercing voice, "And Heeere's Julia!"

A petite gray-haired woman in a demure silk print dress stepped up to the microphone.

"You may not believe this," she began in a clear, dry voice. "But I'm just doing comedy until I can start my own travel agency. I have some great ideas for really innovative tours. For example, why not a cruise for hypochondriacs on the medical ship *Plague*? In addition to dining and dancing with the world's best doctors, you'd get one free physical and one minor surgery as part of your fare. There'd be digital thermometers in every cabin, evening lectures on the world's most disgusting diseases, and lessons on how to say 'I'm sick' in twenty different languages."

A single loud guffaw echoed in the half-empty room. It came from Romney Baxter, who finally had looked up from the yellow pad and was staring at the sixty-five-year-old lady comic with admiration.

Mia shook her head as if to clear it. She couldn't believe her eyes. Her own shy, conventional mother was standing up on the stage telling jokes. Her mind simply couldn't absorb the astonishing fact.

"And if you think I'm not serious about this idea, just ask my daughter over there." Julia gave Mia a big wave. "Hello, doll. Don't clap. I couldn't stand the noise."

The audience joined Romney with a few laughs.

"Well, where are you taking me for dinner?" Before Boyd could say anything more, he felt a sharp blow to his shins.

"I'm going to get even with you for this if it's the last thing I do," Mia whispered.

"Hey, be reasonable, Mia. You came of your own free will. We had a bet."

"Well, all bets are off. My mother has the right to perform in a comedy club without being subjected to your wild accusations concerning your father." Mia swallowed hard. Julia had just delivered another punch line in her prissy, high-pitched teacher's voice and again only one now-familiar laugh was heard in the room.

Mia was assaulted by a shower of emotions, all of which pierced and hurt like arrows. She was angry with Boyd for causing her distress, unreasonably it was true, but that didn't quiet her rage. She was proud of her prim and proper gray-haired mother having the courage to get up there on stage and perform—but mostly she was worried. Surely it couldn't be good for an elderly lady with a weak heart to be up so late, exerting herself in the unhealthy atmosphere of the Laff-A-Minute.

She watched anxiously as Julia, undaunted by the lack of laughs and applause, went on from one joke to another, her eyes twinkling behind her old-fashioned harlequin glasses, a happy smile on her face. Mia wished more than anything in the world that she could put her arms around her mother's frail shoulders and protect her from the unappreciative audience.

Audience! Mia glanced at Mary Goudge. The woman's face was set in grim, disapproving lines. She had met Julia Taylor at a library reception and knew she was Mia's mother.

Mia looked again at her mother, trying now to see

her through Mary Goudge's eyes. She had to admit that the sight of a senior citizen trying to be a stand-up comic *was* ridiculous. Mia felt a flash of shame at her mother's inappropriate behavior.

Then she caught herself. Since when were Mary Goudge's standards *hers*? Since never! Embarrassment wasn't the issue. It was her mother's health she was concerned about.

Besides the fact that she obviously was enjoying herself, why was Julia risking her health for such a meager reward? Mia wondered. Knowing her spirited, indomitable mother—the woman who had put herself through college when her husband died so she could support her daughter—Mia decided it was the challenge that attracted Julia to that bare, ugly stage. There was nothing harder than making people laugh. Somehow Julia must have overcome her fear of public speaking.

There was a sprinkling of polite applause punctuated like cannon shot by Romney's loud clapping. Julia stepped away from the microphone to make room for the emcee.

"You've got to give Julia a lot of credit. She keeps coming back, so I'm sure we'll see her again, folks. And just let me remind you aspiring comics out there that there's no limit on the number of times you can try out at Laff-A-Minute. If you're willing to take a chance, so are we."

Julia walked demurely off the stage and stood hesitatingly between Romney's table and Mia's.

Romney got up and clasped both her hands in his. His voice boomed out, almost drowning the timid opening jokes of the next comic. "You were magnificent, Julia. I'll bet Lily Tomlin is shaking in her boots. That new material . . ." Putting his large, veiny hand around her small waist, he led Julia to his table.

Mia glanced at Boyd to see how he was reacting. Not well, she thought. His handsome, aquiline nose looked pinched and puritanical. His mouth was arrow-straight.

"Now do you see what I mean? Your mother has my father wrapped around her little finger."

"From what I can see, *your* father has *his* arm wrapped around *my* mother's waist."

Boyd glared at her. "*I* think you should take this more seriously. Don't you see *each* of them is bad for the *other*? They abet each other in their crazy, unbecoming escapades. He writes her material, and she performs it week after week in this crummy club. They seem to have lost all idea of decorum and propriety, even decency."

"Isn't *decency* going a bit far?" Mia strove for a reasonable, even humorous tone, but she heard her voice shake and felt her cheeks flush.

Seeing how upset she was, Boyd put his hands gently on Mia's arm. "I think we should go over there and talk to them. Maybe we can dissuade them from this comedy compulsion they seem to have."

Mia jerked her arm away and stood up. She started to go to her mother, but the elderly couple, both beaming with pride, were on their way to Mia and Boyd's table. Mia took a few steps forward to meet them and hugged her mother.

"What did you think, baby?" Julia said. "Were you surprised to see your old mom up there onstage?"

"Surprised isn't the word for it," Mia said diplomatically. With her arm around Julia's thin shoulders, Mia led her mother to a chair. "Sit down, Mom. You must be exhausted."

"Not a bit. I'm having an absolute ball."

Romney clapped Boyd on the shoulder, shook his hand, and said "Son!" in a man-to-man way. Introductions followed, and an exuberant Julia and Romney sat down.

"Wasn't she just great up there?" Romney asked enthusiastically. He looked around at the small audience. "It's a cold house," Romney whispered. "You should have been here last week," he confided to Mia.

"I was here," Boyd said pointedly.

Romney shot Boyd a disapproving glance from under thick white eyebrows that once must have been as dark as his son's. "Julia is a very talented woman. It would be a sin to hold her back."

"I agree that my mother is very talented, but is this the place for her to exercise her talents?" Mia looked around at the bare walls and scuffed-up floor, at the thin wreaths of cigarette smoke snaking their way up to the low ceiling. "It isn't even healthy here."

"Mia's right," Boyd said firmly. "It isn't good for either of you to be hanging around this grungy club. How can you, at your age, Dad, stay out till two or three in the morning, tear around town on a motorcycle, and do Lord knows what else? You'll destroy your health." Boyd's voice broke. "And you're the only dad I've got, dammit."

Mia was moved in spite of herself. Boyd was supporting her in her argument with their parents. At the moment she'd trade every book in the library to see those sharp blue seafarer's eyes soften as he looked at her.

Then she swung her head to the left. It was like a Ping-Pong match, back and forth across the table.

"I appreciate your concern, son, but Julia and I like doing this. We've been coming here for at least a month, and I don't see it affecting our health at all. Comedy's fun. It's a challenge. Julia gets beter every week, and I think my material's improving. Don't you, Julia?"

Julia's eyes shone behind the harlequin glasses as she looked at Romney. "There's never been anything wrong with your material, dear. We just have to educate the public to appreciate it."

"Oh, brother," Boyd muttered under his breath.

Mia stared at her mother. She was in love! She transferred her gaze to Romney Taylor.

Both Julia and Romney had suddenly become intent on the comic onstage. He was getting laughs, and they were listening to every word. Romney kept his pencil poised over the yellow pad, ready to start writing.

Mia whispered to Boyd, "It's your father who seduced my mother. Not the other way around."

Boyd passed his hand wearily over his forehead. "Let's leave aside the question of blame for the moment and try to talk some sense into them. See how bad they look. They're pale and tired, and I'm sure Dad is losing weight."

"Well, to be quite honest," Mia said, "my mother always is a bit pale. But I'm sure they're tired. I know *I* am. You don't have to take me home," Mia added hurriedly. She tapped Julia on the arm. "Mom, can I ride home with you?"

"Well, honey, I'm afraid not. I came on Romney's motorcycle."

"Do you think that's safe? I mean, Romney's—"

"Not young? Oh, but dear, think of all the years of driving experience he's had."

"Listen, you two," Boyd began sternly, "don't you think you should slow down a bit, maybe find other hobbies, something like bingo, or shuffleboard."

Julia and Romney laughed in unison. "Oh no," Julia said, looking mischievously at Romney, "we'd be with all those old fogies who think a ten P.M. TV program is *The Late, Late Show*."

Romney snapped back with "Our get-up-and-go would really have got-up-and-went."

Boyd groaned. "You're hopeless, both of you."

"Come back to the Laff-A-Minute on Thursday and see how *those* jokes go over," Julia said.

"Mo . . . ther!" Mia protested, dragging the two syllables out.

"Look, why don't we all go out for a late supper together," Boyd said, "and continue discussing this over some food and coffee."

"Julia and I usually have a bite at the Zebra Lounge after her routine. The food's not great, but we find a little discoing helps us to unwind after the tension of performing."

"The Zebra Lounge! Discoing!" Mia exclaimed.

"Really, Mia, you sound like an echo," Julia complained.

"That's logical. I feel like I'm being bounced off the wall by you two." Mia's gray eyes widened as she realized what she was saying. "Oh, no, it's hereditary. I, too, could end up as a stand-up comic."

Boyd was the only one who found her remark funny.

Romney glanced meaningfully at Julia. The two

rose as one. "Well, if you two kids don't want to join us, we'll be on our merry way."

"Don't wait up, Mia," Julia called out, tucking her hand in the crook of Romney's arm.

Mia stared after them until the roar of an engine throbbed through the air and died away. Then she turned to Boyd. To her surprise he was still laughing at what she had said.

Mia noticed details about him she had missed before, especially the way his eyes narrowed to aquamarine slits between his long, sooty lashes.

He was a dirty rat, a family enemy, a male know-it-all. But she couldn't convince her body! It was racing down its own track—her pulse pounding, lips going soft and pouty, and fireworks of need exploding deep inside her.

The whole scene was driving her crazy. She couldn't take any more.

Mia stood up abruptly. "Please take me home, Boyd. It's late and I'm tired."

"You owe me a dinner," Boyd said with mock seriousness.

"Two A.M. is a little late for the best dinner in town."

"Suppose I let you off cheap. I know an all-night coffee shop that serves the kind of apple pie Mom used to make." He paused. "Before she became a stand-up comic."

He got the effect he wanted. Mia laughed. And in Boyd's book, anything you could laugh at you could survive. He knew that from experience.

"You sold me. I love apple pie."

"Peach, strawberry, blueberry, boysenberry, chocolate cream, and pecan," the elderly waitress with the name tag *Debbie* on the orange and white striped uniform intoned wearily.

"Apple," Boyd answered.

"We got only one piece of apple left."

"*You* take it," Boyd urged Mia. "I like strawberry just as much."

"No, you. It's my treat, and you're my guest, remember."

Boyd shook his head. "No way. You *love* apple pie. You said so."

Mia looked doubtful.

"Listen, I haven't got all night," Debbie complained, leaning her body against the table. "Suppose I bring one piece of apple pie and two forks?"

"Fine," Boyd said happily. "And two cups of coffee. All right, Mia?"

Mia nodded. The bright lights of the coffee shop seemed to have jolted her awake. Or was it the way Boyd looked at her as he moved closer, his eyes weaving a bond between them, claiming her as his own?

Mia's hand fell open, palm up. Boyd took it in his. "It's too bad we had to meet like this. Enemies." He planted a kiss in the heart of her soft palm.

Every nerve in her body quivered as his open, moist mouth touched her tender skin. Unconsciously she cupped her hand as though to hold the kiss forever.

"The Montagues and the Capulets," she murmured.

Boyd raised his head. "With an overage Romeo and Juliet."

Just then Debbie reappeared. "Well?"

Boyd put Mia's hand back on the table as if it were a precious piece of porcelain. Debbie plunked one huge slab of pie and two forks in the center of the table and left.

Boyd cut into the pie and held out a bite-size morsel to Mia. "One fork would have been enough."

The intimacy implicit in the gesture started a train of fantasies in Mia's mind of his tongue skimming along the underside of her lips, his hard mouth closing over hers, her lips parting instantly.

No man—not even Gary—had aroused her as Boyd Baxter was, and she had only just met him. It was silly, but she felt if she took that bite of apple pie, she'd be a goner. They'd be exchanging cinammon-scented kisses as soon as they got to the car. Then what would happen to her mother? To her?

Mia gently steered the fork with the tempting tid-bit back toward Boyd. With her fork she divided the slab of pie in two.

"That's your territory. This is mine."

Boyd narrowed his aquamarine eyes knowingly at her. He raised his fork vertically in the air. "Pistols at dawn?"

Mia glanced at her watch. "That would make it in about an hour."

"Well, then, shall we talk? We have to decide what we are going to do about keeping our wayward parents at home, out of smoke-filled cellars, off danger-ous motorcycles, away from discos, and safely in bed at ten."

"I'm all for it. You may not know this, but Mom had a mild heart attack some years ago, which is why I'm living at home. I don't think tearing around on a motorcycle can be doing her heart any good." Mia probed meditatively at her piece of apple pie. "I take it you think they're a bad influence on each other and should be kept apart."

"Well, no, not kept apart but kept out of the Laff-A-Minute. It's giving them *too* much zest for living."

"If my mom keeps bombing the way she did tonight, pretty soon she won't even make amateur night."

"Hmmm. And what's making her bomb?"

"Your dad's jokes," Mia answered.

"Suppose they got worse?"

"They couldn't."

"Oh, I don't know about that." Boyd was smiling, his eyes sparkling.

"You look like Edison discovering the hundred watt bulb," Mia commented. "What's on your mind?"

"Suppose I slipped a sheet of the most awful jokes anyone ever heard in among Dad's papers, and he gave it to your mom along with the other jokes."

"I thought he wrote them in longhand on a yellow pad."

Boyd shook his head. "That's for his comments on the other comics. He types out Julia's material."

Mia's face lit up. "Then Mom would get even fewer laughs than she got tonight. They'd get discouraged and stop going to the comedy club. No late hours, no disco, and probably no motorcycle." Her slim dark brows suddenly met in a frown. "Is it right, though, to interfere in their lives?"

"It's for their own good, Mia. If we don't stop them now, they'll be doing all their dating in a hospital corridor. They're really endangering their safety and their health."

"Okay, do it!" Mia said firmly. "And I'll help you with the jokes."

Boyd leaned forward and cradled Mia's face in his long fingers. "You know, you've got a genuine talent for comedy. Maybe I can get you in the Laff-A-Minute."

Mia threw her head back and laughed.

The sight sent a charge of high-voltage pleasure through Boyd. Deciding that the only way to get rid of temptation was to yield to it, he bent his lips to Mia's half-opened ones and brushed them back and forth with feather-light caresses.

There was a rustle of a starched skirt at the table.

"Here's your check," Debbie said flatly. "Pay at the cash register."

Slowly, reluctantly, Boyd pulled away from Mia. "I'll call you tomorrow."

Her gray, dark-fringed eyes widened. Boyd thought he could read her thoughts in their clear, limpid depths. She was wondering whether it was a good idea to see him again.

"We have to stay on top of the situation," he said firmly. "Otherwise what will happen to them?"

She was still in the thrall of his kiss. Her head swam, her lips felt poised for more.

Or to *us*? Mia asked herself. Would it be better if she backed off from this much-too-attractive man right now?

But did she have the right to desert her mother in her hour of need? Mia had a flash of a mental picture of Julia discoing away in some jolly, slightly disreputable club, exchanging one-liners with Romney Baxter. More to the point, would Julia even *want* to be rescued?

"I suppose if we left them alone, they'd just go on having a good time," Mia answered.

"Sometimes you have to do things for people's own good," Boyd said virtuously.

Visualizing her mother clutching the elderly waist of Romney Baxter on the back of a speeding motorcycle, Mia said, "One has to do one's duty, doesn't one?"

Boyd agreed. "Duty before pleasure."

In that case, Mia wondered, what was the reason for the kiss?

Two

"How's the stew, dear?"

"Delicious, Mom. You really outdid yourself this time."

The stew was fragrant with spices and the rich red Burgundy wine Julia had marinated the meat in, and Mia was hungry. Between the children's story hour and a meeting of the library board, she had had time to eat only half a tuna sandwich all day.

Struck by an idea, Mia put her spoon down and looked across the table at her mother. "You're such a good cook, have you ever thought of giving adult education classes in cooking? It would be a challenge, and you wouldn't be endangering your health the way you are at the Laff-A-Minute."

Julia's face fell.

"Romney could be your assistant," Mia said quickly. "He could write your lesson plans." Her voice warmed with enthusiasm. "It's a great idea. I bet the two of you would end up on TV. *Cooking with Julia and Romney.*"

Julia shook her head. "I couldn't *teach* cooking, dear. I don't even use a recipe. I just add a pinch of something here and a pinch of something else there. I'll grant you the results are usually good, but it's all intuitive."

Well, Mia thought, that was one idea shot down. She started eating again.

"What made you think of becoming a stand-up comic?" Mia asked with a puzzled expression. "It doesn't seem like the sort of thing you would do."

Her voice vibrant and eager, Julia answered, "I'll tell you how I got started. You remember, I always liked to tell jokes to my students. Well, my fellow teachers urged me to try out at Laff-A-Minute. I did about a month ago and just loved it, and I've been going once or twice a week ever since, every time they have amateur night."

"But Mom, you didn't get a rousing reception last night. Aren't you discouraged?"

"Honey, if I could survive my first six months as a teacher, I can survive anything."

"Why didn't you tell me you were going to the Laff-A-Minute instead of lying about playing bridge?" Mia asked in a hurt tone. "Did you think I wouldn't understand?"

"Oh, I didn't doubt that you would understand. I just wanted to wait until I had made it big before letting anyone—even you—know. Some members of the library board are so conservative." Julia made a face. "I saw Mary Goudge at the club last night."

"I saw her today too," Mia said ruefully. "She made some catty remark about "astounding performance,"" and made it clear that she was at the club only because her out-of-town guests had wanted to go there."

Julia's hand flew to her lips. "Oh my dear, she wouldn't hold back your promotion or have you fired, would she?"

Mia got up and put her arms around her mother. "Don't you *dare* worry about me, Mom. I can handle Mary Goudge. Besides, she and her stuffy friends are in the minority on the board."

Giving her mother an extra little squeeze, Mia returned to her seat and started eating again.

After a while she looked up and asked, "How about Romney? Where'd you meet him?"

Julia laughed a little and got up from the table. "Speaking of Romney, I'll get the dessert."

"Mother!" Mia said with a laugh.

"Well, Romney is the dessert at the end of my life. And I don't mean rice pudding either," Julia added as she carried a three-layer fudge cake to the table.

"At least he hasn't interfered with your cooking," Mia said, amused.

"Far from *interfering* with anything, Romney has enhanced my life immeasurably. Your father's been gone fifteen long years. You're grown up. What was I supposed to do with my life when I retired—play bridge night and day? You know a sedentary life is bad for the heart."

"Okay, Mom, you win. Now where did you meet the luscious hunk of cake?" Mia stared dumbfounded at the alternating tiers of dark chocolate and coffee-colored mocha frosting on her plate. "I mean, how did you make this luscious cake?"

"A Freudian slip, dear. Don't let it bother you.

Romney was taking an adult education comedy-writing class and used to go to the clubs to learn more about the art. The first time I performed at the Laff-A-Minute, he came up afterward to congratulate me and asked if I'd like to see some of his material. We started working together, then dating, and now we're . . . well, an item, as the gossip columnists used to say."

"Well, as an item, Boyd and I wish you two would engage in healthier activities."

"Boyd's awfully handsome and nice, Mia. And he's attracted to you, I can tell. Do you like him?" Julia asked.

"Mother, we were talking about you and Romney."

"Oh, Romney and I are just a pair of golden oldies having our last fling. But you're only twenty-seven. You have your whole life ahead of you, Mia. Just because—"

"Just because I was left at the church once doesn't mean it will happen again. In fact, the chances of its happening again are about the same, I'd say, as being hit twice by lightning."

The bright glow of inner happiness had faded from Julia's face. "I don't know what went wrong, how Gary could do such a thing! Why he didn't even let you know!" Julia shuddered. "It was horrible—that little clock in the dressing room ticking away while I hurried to get those rows and rows of tiny cloth-covered buttons on your beautiful wedding dress done up. And then the waiting while the organ played everything but the wedding march until finally your Uncle John had to get up and make the announcement."

"Please, Mom," Mia begged, "don't keep going over

and over it. Gary probably just got cold feet and was too ashamed to tell me. He left town immediately afterward, remember."

"You handled the situation very courageously, Mia."

Mia smiled ruefully. "Oh, it hurt, but I got over it. The incident did leave a few scars. Maybe I'm a little more leery of men than I used to be, but, as you know, that hasn't kept me from dating. I just haven't found Mr. Right yet. I'm still looking," she added gaily.

Julia nodded with conviction. "You'll find him, Mia. No question about it."

"But when I do, Mom, I want you there to do up all those hundreds of buttons again. Frankly I'm seriously concerned about your well-being. Staying out late every night and performing in smoke-filled rooms can't be good for your heart. To say nothing of the danger in tearing around town on a motorcycle."

"Mia, my ambition to be a stand-up comic has given purpose and challenge to my life, and even a little excitement—rare qualities when you're old. I know inside me that I have the talent to succeed at comedy, but like everyone else I have to start at the bottom, and that means smoke-filled rooms and late hours. As for the motorcycle, I assure you I feel perfectly safe with Romney."

Mia shook her head. "I don't agree, Mom, but I'm not going to quarrel with you about it." She rose and carried the dishes to the sink. "I'll load the dishwasher. I brought a video home from the library. It's a suspense film. Why don't we watch it together?"

After Mia had rinsed off the dishes and slotted them into the dishwasher, she and Julia sat down o watch the movie. But Mia found her thoughts drifting immediately to Boyd.

What was he doing tonight? Was he out with someone? She pictured him helping a luscious redhead in a designer evening gown into the sleek black Lamborghini.

Mia decided to run *that* film backward, like the old movie comedies where the man jumps out of the swimming pool back onto the diving board. She had Boyd open the car door and hustle the redhead out. Then he drove away. Mia certainly didn't care if the redhead was left standing on the sidewalk, staring disconsolately at the disappearing car.

Mia forced her attention back to the screen, but thoughts of Boyd won out again. She could still taste his kiss, remember how his lips had felt on hers, warm and firm and tempting. Boyd Baxter could easily tempt her into situations she didn't want to be in. So she should hope that he *was* out with another woman, she decided.

"Pass the popcorn, dear," Julia said, her eyes glued to the screen. "Isn't it exciting?"

"Yes, he is," Mia answered, recalling the sexual intensity in Boyd's striking blue eyes, the sensuality of his deep laugh, the gentle yet thrilling way he had of touching her.

"Very." Boyd exuded power from his broad shoulders to his long runner's legs. But there was power, too, in the confident swing of his walk, in his low, self-assured voice, in his success.

Julia had a mother's psychic antenna, Mia determined. Over a mouthful of popcorn, she mumbled, "Boyd Baxter's a real catch, dear."

"Mom," Mia said wearily, "watch the movie."

• • •

Boyd looked down at the long yellow pad proppe
up on his knee and chuckled. He had to have wri
ten the worst jokes ever. If Julia Taylor got even or
laugh with his jokes, outside of his dad's loud gu
faws, there was no future in America for comedy, h
thought.

He started to write again, then stopped, lost i
another world. He closed his eyes, remembering th
feel of Mia's velvety skin when he caressed her han
the sweet floral scent of her perfume, the soft yiel
ing of her lips under his.

Boyd threw the legal pad on the floor and spran
out of his easy chair. He thrust his hands in hi
pockets and started pacing the living room floor.

He had said he'd call her, but should he? Wh
needed complex, interesting women? He had alread
lived through one complicated relationship in hi
life, and it had hurt like hell.

The woman he had loved and lived with for a yea
had decided to go back to her ex-husband becaus
he needed her more than Boyd did. Jeanne was tha
kind of woman. She had to be needed.

Boyd had tried to dissuade Jeanne for her ow
sake as well as his. But Jeanne had felt drawn to th
other, weaker man for reasons she hadn't fully fath
omed herself. The equal partnership Boyd envisione
in a relationship had not been what Jeanne reall
wanted.

Boyd paced some more, then he wheeled aroun
and strode to the phone as though attacking i
Damn! He wanted to be with Mia, and only Mia. N
one else would do. She was vibrant and vital, a
individual with a rich personality, the woman h

was drawn to. He could spend the rest of his life watching the deep dimple come and go in her cheek. Her low, musical laugh laid a fire trail of desire along his nerves. Every time she tossed back her head, he wanted to kiss her swanlike white throat, to press his lips to her pulses and feel them tremble with excitement.

Thinking of her, Boyd knew he couldn't wait. He had to be with Mia. He punched a series of numbers on the touch-tone phone and waited.

Listening to the phone ring at the other end, Boyd told himself she wasn't home, and felt his heart take a nosedive. Then Mia's cool, sweet voice said "Hello" and he broke into a smile.

"Mia, this is Boyd, and I need help."

"Who doesn't?"

"I mean special help, something that concerns you and me. Are you free to talk?"

"No, the phone's being tapped by the National Comedy Commission. Of course I can talk. What can I do for you?"

"I don't suppose you'd like it if I growled 'Plenty, Baby' under my breath."

"Boyd, if you can growl 'Plenty, Baby,' *you* should go on the stage."

"Which brings us to the point of why I'm calling."

"I'm ready," Mia said humorously.

"I've got a page of really bad jokes. Want to hear them?"

"Not over the phone." Mia lowered her voice. "Mother's here."

"How about coming over to my condo. I'll pick you up."

There was a long silence. "Come hear my really

bad jokes sounds like a variation on an old theme: 'Come up and see my etchings.' "

"You can see my etchings another time, Mia. Tonight all I can offer are bad jokes."

She laughed, and Boyd pictured her smooth, ebony pageboy swinging as she tilted her head back. He was overcome with the desire to thrust his face behind her dark curtain of hair and kiss her perfectly shaped ear, to nibble gently at it and taste with his tongue the sweet flowery scent she used.

"I'll be there right away, Mia."

"I'll be ready." She hoped as she hung up the phone.

Every contact with Boyd left her bothered and bewildered. She couldn't sort out the feelings he aroused in her. Heady excitement surged through her body, making her poignantly aware of her femininity. At the same time, she didn't want to be swept away by her emotions. She needed to take it slowly, to give the relationship time.

Always present, nagging at her mind, too, was anxiety about her mother. Romney and his motorcycle were very much to blame for her concern, and Mia couldn't be sure that she and Boyd would see eye to eye over controlling their problem parents.

Boyd's condo was in a discreetly elegant building overlooking the harbor. The entire rear wall of the living room was glass with a view of fairylike beauty. The shifting lights of the yachts riding at anchor shimmered on the dark water, while the homes on the shore across the way shone their light steadily into the clear, dark night.

"It's lovely," Mia said simply.

"The view *is* terrific," Boyd agreed.

"I didn't mean just the view. I meant the room too. I like the colors—the soft off-white with the splashes of brown and burnt orange. And the comfortable furniture. *And* the books."

She opened her eyes wide and pursed her lips in a gentle, mocking smile. It was an utterly ravishing smile. Boyd couldn't take his gaze from it. Her full lower lip, protruding ever so slightly over the delicately sculpted upper one, had a roguish, impudent allure. He ran his tongue over his own lips and moved closer.

"If I show you my library card, can we get to know each other better?"

"Sir! I'll have you know librarians don't make deals." Mia said haughtily.

Boyd smirked. "I heard librarians do it between the covers."

Laughing, Mia moved away from the picture window. "Which reminds me of why I was invited here." Realizing what she had said, Mia blushed and her laugh went a little higher. "I mean, where are those really bad jokes of yours?"

"Over here." Boyd indicated the oversized coffee table between the beige leather sofa and the black marble fireplace where flames danced restlessly behind brass-trimmed glass doors. A yellow legal pad rested beside a built-in chessboard with the intricately carved black and white pieces already in place.

Mia smiled with pleasure. "Looks like you're a real chess enthusiast."

"My dad and I always play when he comes over. Do you play?"

Mia nodded. "Yes, but it's been years. My dad taught me. I don't play very often though."

"Suppose I challenge you to a game. We can go over the jokes after."

"Loser pays for another piece of apple pie at the all-night coffee shop?"

"Let's decide on the stakes later." Boyd arched his eyebrows in a mock leer. "I'm sure we can think of something more interesting than apple pie. Why don't you sit on the couch, and I'll pull up a chair opposite you."

As Mia took a seat on the couch, Boyd's gaze roamed over her velvety skin. The fire's rosy reflection touched the swell of one ivory breast, which was exposed under her deeply cut white silk blouse when she moved a certain way. The chess game would give him more time to look at her, he thought, to listen to the trill of her low, infectious laughter, to keep her with him a little longer.

Mia caught his look. It was as if Boyd were undressing her with his gaze. Mia felt a flutter in her stomach. Her pulses pounded in her ears. She became overwhelmingly aware of Boyd's maleness. His big hands rested by the chessboard ready to move a piece. A somewhat darker cloud of soft chest hair was visible in the open neck of his silk sport shirt. She visualized the toasty brown curls running across his flat stomach, and . . . She'd better concentrate on chess, she told herself.

"As I remember, white goes first," she said, moving one of her pawns forward two squares.

"Right," Boyd said, as he pushed his black pawn forward. "I think I should warn you I play an aggressive game."

"And I'm pretty good at defense."

What game were they referring to? Mia wondered. If it was chess, she was out to capture his chessmen. If it was love, she was in danger of being captured herself.

How ironic it was to be playing an intellectual game such as chess with sexual tension crackling between them like lightning in a thunderstorm!

As the game progressed, it was obvious that Boyd was the better player. He already had captured several white pawns, Mia's knight, and a rook.

"My dad taught me how to play when I was just a kid," he said apologetically. "My mother was ill for many years with Parkinson's disease, so Dad and I would while away the evenings playing chess when I didn't have homework to do."

"What happened to your mother?" Mia asked sympathetically.

"She died about ten years ago. Dad was really broken up over it. We became very close, which may be why I'm so protective of him. I mean, he's been through a lot. Anyway, we started playing chess again because it took his mind off Mom's death."

"I'm sorry about your mother," Mia said sincerely.

"Dad's all right now, and so am I. I'm glad he enjoys your mom's company. I think she's a great lady with all the spunk in the world. I don't want to see anything happen to either of them."

Mia shuddered. "Every time I think of that motorcycle—"

"Or the Laff-A-Minute. I don't think the owner ever airs the place out. You could get lung cancer just stepping through the front door."

"And discoing! When Mom talks about the Zebra

Lounge, all I can think about is her getting a slipped disc."

Boyd moved his queen dangerously close to Mia's king. "I guess you're an only child too."

"That's right, and a California native to boot."

Boyd grinned. "A rare species."

As Boyd pondered his next move, Mia said, "I don't want to distract you, but . . ."

Boyd looked up from the chessboard and let his gaze travel appreciatively over the ripe swell of her breasts. "Distract me! It's a miracle I can even play chess."

Mia flushed a little. "I was going to ask you if you remembered *Alice Through the Looking Glass.*"

"I like the ending when Alice wakes up and shakes her kitten, thinking it's a chess piece, the Red Queen," Boyd said.

Mia stared into the fire for a moment, musing. "At the end Alice wonders who really dreamed it all. The Red King was part of her dream, of course, but then she was part of his dream too."

She felt drawn to return her gaze to Boyd and looked directly into his eyes. There was a certain dreaminess in the aquamarine depths that matched her own feelings.

Were she and Boyd part of each other's dream? Were they meant for each other? Mia gave her head a little shake. It was too soon to tell. She had learned from experience that life was unpredictable. You didn't always know how things would turn out, and it was useless to speculate.

She forced her attention back to the chessboard. "I think it's your move."

Boyd moved his knight to join his queen in a

threatening position against Mia's king. "Check!" he called out triumphantly.

"Oh, no!" Mia wailed, studying the board.

"And checkmate," Boyd said gently, "There's no way your king can escape capture."

"You're right," Mia said, smiling. "I surrender."

"You played a good game, Mia. I'll give you a rematch any time you say." He saw Mia's glance stray to the antique clock on the marble mantel. He couldn't bear to have her leave yet. It seemed to him that he could never get enough of watching the subtle changes of expression on her vivacious face, listening to her lilting laugh, being close to the sweet warmth of her lovely body. "You'd better look at those jokes I wrote for your mother," he said hurriedly. "That's why you came, remember?"

"I'll look them over quickly. It's getting late, Boyd."

"Can I get you anything to drink?"

"A Perrier would be lovely."

"Coming right up. In the meantime you can be looking at the material I wrote." He slid the legal pad over to Mia.

She was still reading when he returned with two tall glasses of mineral water.

"Well, what do you think?" Boyd asked as he handed her a glass and sat down on the couch beside her. "If you agree that the jokes really stink, I'll type them up and slip them into Dad's portfolio."

"They're great," Mia answered. "I mean, they're really bad. It's a mean, low-down trick. But when Mom doesn't get a laugh with these jokes, she and Romney might quit the comedy business and stay home nights."

"I'm glad you approve." Boyd raised his glass. "To us!"

Mia clinked glasses with him. "To comedy! Or rather, noncomedy!"

"Will you compromise on *romantic* comedy?"

"You make it sound like *The Late Show* our folks are too hip to watch," Mia said wryly. Were they getting into dangerous territory, mentioning their parents? She hoped not. It was so pleasant, sitting with Boyd in front of the fire, making light conversation. They were friends, but not just friends, because there was a sexual spark between them. She couldn't help but be aware of his tight jeans on his long muscular legs, the tingling warmth of his fingers as he handed her the glass and touched her hand.

Mia sighed and looked into the fire.

"What are you thinking of?" he asked quietly, putting his arm around her shoulders.

"How nice it is that we're getting along instead of quarreling. I'm really quite a peaceable person."

"So am I. I prefer reasoning with somebody to fighting him. If the other guy's as reasonable as I am," Boyd added, joking. "And look how much we have in common. We're California-born champion chess players who love old movies and have problem parents and no siblings."

Mia threw her head back and laughed.

Boyd's control snapped. He had held out long enough. He couldn't resist the beauty of her throat, the graceful long curve of it, the creamy softness.

He kissed her on the side of her neck and let his lips linger there. He nibbled a bit, his strong white teeth gentle and yet wild in his hunger for her. Then he laved the soft skin with his tongue.

Mia shivered. Her whole body was throbbing. She was aware of nothing but the warmth radiating from him and the heady male scent that drugged her senses. The feel of his velvety tongue against her neck was exotically different from anything she had ever experienced before. It was incredibly, excitingly delightful.

She leaned back against the soft cushions, arching her back, giving herself up to him. Bending down, he brushed her eyelids with his lips as his fingers toyed with the curving bell of her ebony pageboy. The stroking sensation lulled Mia into a near-hypnotic state that made her feel as if her whole body were melting.

Boyd caught her face between his rough palms and held her still as he twisted his hard, hungry mouth against hers. Her lips parted instantly to allow his tongue to probe within. His hands moved lower, slipping down to trace the curve of her shoulder.

Mia could feel the unmistakable need, the hard promise in every line of Boyd's body as he leaned over her, and a very primitive part of her thrilled to it. Her fingertips, which had been splayed in feeble, unmeant protest against his chest, lifted to curl into the thickness of his rich chestnut hair.

Caught up in the vortex of passion Boyd was unleashing, she couldn't think coherently, couldn't get her bearings long enough even to find reality. All she wanted was to obey the passionate, timeless call of her senses. She wanted to give herself completely to Boyd Baxter.

Boyd took the lobe of her ear gently between his teeth and tugged at it, and a flicker of liquid heat rose between her thighs. He seemed happy just to play with her ear, to plant kisses in the vulnerable area behind the lobe, and to nuzzle it as his hands described to her in thrilling gestures the landscape of her own body.

The warmth of the fire relaxed her. Boyd's caresses and the seductive scent of his musky after-shave were exciting her to the point of delirium. Mia locked her arms around his neck. Then, tempted by the curly strands of hair visible under his silk shirt, let her hands drift downward to tangle in the tufts.

"Oh, Mia, you delectable thing," Boyd murmured against her lips. She stretched out luxuriously, her leather miniskirt riding up even further on her legs.

A ship's bell rang somewhere out in the harbor. The sound jarred her free of the world of sensual chaos she had drifted into. It awakened the thought, sharp and clear in her consciousness, that going to bed with Boyd was not something she really wanted to do. She sat up abruptly and said, "Boyd, please take me home."

"Are you sure?" he asked thickly.

"Yes, I'm sure."

Boyd watched Mia as she straightened her skirt and patted down her hair. She had regained her composure—that sweet coolness with which she met the world, but a creamy rosiness still tinted her cheeks. Her chest was heaving a little under her blouse, her nipples pressing against the thin cloth.

Boyd inhaled sharply and turned away, unable to stand the throbbing need that rose within him again. It was the fire and ice quality of hers that drove him wild. It thrilled him to think he was the only one who knew the passion that lay below her cool surface.

But she had made the right decision, he thought. Their chances of a meaningful relationship could be ruined if they went to bed together so soon. He didn't want only a sexual relationship with Mia. She was a woman he wanted to know, to enjoy, to savor. Time was on their side, time and circumstances. Hadn't they pledged themselves to the goal of helping their parents?

By the time Boyd got home, the fire had burned down to a rosy glow. He sat on the couch and picked up the legal pad that was still on the glass-topped table. Then he studied the jokes he had written.

There was no doubt about it. They were old-fashioned and unfunny. They would kill Julia's act for sure.

But he wasn't satisfied. Some unresolved doubt nagged at the back of his mind. Jokes were supposed to be funny. He had spent his whole life doing things the right way. It was a violation of his own standards to deliberately undertake something that would fail. Purposely writing unfunny jokes was like throwing a basketball game or buying property you knew was worthless.

Boyd read through the material again, and his feeling of uneasiness grew. Decisively, as he did everything, he ripped the yellow sheet off the pad, crumpled it up, and threw it on the floor. He drew the pad toward him. Pencil poised in the air, he stared into the dying fire.

Then he started to write furiously. He covered

page after page with his strong, sloping hand writing. Suddenly tired, he threw the pencil down.

The fire was out. Its absence made the room chilly.

Boyd read the jokes aloud to hear how they sounded. They were much better than the previous ones, he decided. They were more contemporary, sharper, with stronger punch lines.

He felt good inside for having done the right thing. Mia might be disappointed, but Boyd was sure that when he told her, she'd understand.

Three

Mia stroked her hand along the door of the Lamborghini as Boyd opened it for her.

A barely suppressed grin turned up the corners of his lips. "It likes to be scratched behind the ears too."

Mia was embarrassed at having been caught in such a silly act of affection. "I don't think I could reach behind the fenders," she said.

From behind the steering wheel, Boyd inclined his head toward her. "Try my fenders," he teased.

Going along with the gag, Mia ran her fingers lightly behind Boyd's right ear. The gesture seemed especially sweet and intimate. It was sensual too— Mia could feel a tingle inside her that was very pleasant but not something she wanted to indulge. They had a long evening ahead of them. It was an evening Mia had looked forward to, because Boyd was so much fun. He made her feel silly and happy and excited all at the same time. But she had no intention of inviting another delicious assault on her senses like the one she'd enjoyed so much in his condo.

Mia withdrew her hand, but not before a low chesty noise began to emanate from Boyd.

"Is that you or the car?" Mia asked.

"Me. I'm purring. If you scratch me under the chin, I'll roll over for you."

Mia pretended alarm. "Not in heavy traffic!"

"Then we'll save it for later," Boyd said confidently as he expertly pulled the Lamborghini up to the curb in front of the Laff-A-Minute.

There was a scattering of people at the round metal tables in the cavernous room. Streams of cigarette smoke drifted upward to mingle with the stale air. Mia couldn't wait to get her mother out of the unhealthy atmosphere.

"There's Dad," Boyd said quietly. "Let's go over and say hello to him."

Boyd laid his hand affectionately on Romney's stooped back. "How's it going, Dad?" He searched the familiar wrinkled face for a sign that his father had discovered that Julia's repertoire included jokes he hadn't himself written. Boyd had assumed all along that Romney wouldn't catch on. His Dad had become a little absent-minded. A life of retirement didn't demand the sharp wits that a business career did.

But Romney's serene blue eyes and ready smile reassured Boyd. He evidently had gotten away with his little trick.

"Just fine, son. How are you tonight, Mia?"

"Very well, thank you, Mr. Baxter."

"I think you're going to enjoy your Mom's show

tonight." Romney thumped the manila folder in front of him. "Got some real good material here."

Boyd glanced sharply at his father. But there was no mischievous twinkle in the older man's eyes, and his smile was one of pride, not irony.

Mia, too, stared at the beige folder. All her hopes for getting her mother out of the Laff-A-Minute rested on it. The page of bad jokes Boyd had inserted would be the means of accomplishing their goal. How smart Boyd was to think of it!

"You won't have long to wait either," Romney added. "Julia's going on early tonight." He winked. "Seniority."

Boyd pulled a chair out for Mia. "Mind if we join you, Dad?"

"I don't want to seem inhospitable, but this is a business operation for Julia and me. I like to concentrate on each comedian, to pick up pointers on style, gestures, facial expressions. You get the picture."

"Oh sure, Dad. I understand. Maybe we can get together after Julia's act."

But Romney wasn't listening. The first comic was clutching the microphone. Romney drew his yellow legal pad toward him and started writing.

"I feel sorry for your dad," Mia said, as Boyd seated her at another table. "And my mother too. Their hopes are really going to be dashed tonight. I have to keep reminding myself that it's for their own good."

Now was the time, Boyd thought, to tell Mia that the jokes she was going to hear wouldn't be as bad as she expected. But just then a young waitress approached their table.

'What'll you have?" she asked.

Boyd ordered a glass of wine for each of them. As the waitress drifted away from the table, Julia appeared onstage.

"Hey, here's Mom!" Mia exclaimed. "Boy, she really is on early tonight."

Boyd thought Mia looked tense and apprehensive. He only would be adding to her burden if he told her the truth about the jokes now. So instead he leaned forward and folded his hand protectively over hers. "How do you feel?"

"Even my butterflies have butterflies. I want her to fail, but I don't think I can stand to watch it happen."

Boyd squeezed her hand sympathetically. He hated to see her suffer. And for all he knew, Julia might bomb even with his material. Comedy was the toughest of all the arts. One man's laugh was another's bored, openmouthed yawn.

But Julia was getting laughs! he realized. Ripples of laughter circled the room after each gag. A few times Julia even had to wait for the laughter to subside before launching into her next bit.

Boyd listened intently. They were his jokes; there was no mistake about it.

He glanced at Mia to see how she was reacting. She was staring wide-eyed at the slight figure on the stage. Furrowing her finely arched brows, she brushed a wing of ebony hair away from her forehead, as though to clarify her vision.

Turning to Boyd, she said accusingly, "They'e laughing!"

Now he really had to tell her. "Mia," he started. But she put her finger to her lips. "Later, please, Boyd. I want to listen to Mom."

Boyd settled down with Mia to listen to Julia's jokes. Not all the gags got laughs, he noticed, Some did and some didn't.

Boyd soon saw that someone—Romney or Julia—had been clever enough to mix his good jokes up with the clinkers. Julia used the funny material to grab the audience's attention at the beginning of her act and to give them something to remember at the end.

As Julia finished and spontaneous applause rang through the room, Boyd wondered for the second time that night if Romney knew what he had done, but he dismissed the idea. It was the most natural thing in the world to rearrange material. Comedians did it all the time.

A beaming but humble Julia put her hands together, bowed to the audience, and said "Thank you" over and over again.

The emcee bounced onto the stage. "Wasn't that great? Wasn't she just marvelous?" He stepped back and stared admiringly at the gray-haired woman who looked demure in a lavender print dress and a single strand of pearls. "What a future!" He waggled his finger playfully under Julia's nose. "But remember where you were discovered." He raised his voice to a cheerleader's yell. "At the Laff-A-Minute!"

"I can't believe this," Mia said despairingly. "I'll never get her out of this place now. That's all she needed, one tiny success." She turned to Boyd, "How *could* Romney learn to write such good material in just a few days?"

"Well, . . ." Boyd started, intent on telling her the truth.

Boyd was still collecting his thoughts, trying to

think of the best way to tell Mia when Julia and Romney sashayed over to their table. Julia clasped Mia's hand. "What did you think, babe? I sort of knocked them dead tonight, didn't I?"

Mia managed a weak. "You were great, Mom."

With eyes shining, Julia looked at Romney. "It was Romney's new material that did it."

"*And* your delivery of it," Romney gallantly pointed out.

Boyd's heart sank. It was too late now to tell Mia who had really written Julia's material. Considering how close Mia was to her mother, she might inadvertently tell Julia the truth. Moreover, Romney looked so pleased at Julia's praise, Boyd didn't have the heart to undermine him. If Romney was happy thinking he had written all those funny jokes, Boyd wasn't going to rain on his parade. His dad deserved a little happiness.

But not at the expense of his health. "Well, now that you two have proven that you can do it, you can relax, can't you?" Boyd asked. "I mean, you know, let the comedy bit drop and go in for something else."

"Drop comedy?" Julia and Romney said in unison. "Never!"

Boyd groaned.

Mia muttered under her breath, "Here we go again."

"We're just getting started," Julia said.

"That's right," Romney chimed in. "Once you've had a success, you're on your way. One success leads to another."

Mia cleared her throat. "I don't want to put down your accomplishment tonight, but"—she looked pointedly around the room—"it was a fairly small success, wasn't it?"

"Big or small doesn't matter," Romney said. "Big oaks from little acorns grow."

Mia gave him a hard look. *Could* this guy write funny jokes? "I have to congratulate you, too, Mr. Baxter, on how quickly you sharpened your style. I mean, only a few days ago—"

"I bought some audiocassettes of famous comedians and listened to them. That really helped a lot."

"Dad and Julia, why don't you sit down and have a Coke or something with us to celebrate." Boyd looked around the room, searching for the waitress.

"We can't stay, son." Romney gazed coyly at Julia. "We have other plans."

Mia looked worried. "The Zebra Lounge?"

Julia patted her daughter's cheek. "Maybe. But don't wait up for me."

Hooking one arm through Romney's, her motorcycle helmet under the other, Julia made her way to the exit. Progress was slow as she acknowledged the compliments of her admirers with modest little smiles and disclaiming head shakes.

Soon thereafter the familiar *vroom-vroom* of Romney's motorcycle vibrated through the air.

"I feel sick," Mia said.

Boyd put his head in his hands. "So do I." He realized that unconsciously he was listening for the sound of a crash. He shrugged off his tension as unreasonable. But he also made a promise to himself. He'd find a way to get his dad off that motorcycle for good. He didn't know how he'd to it, but do it he would.

"I don't think I can stand this place another minute," Mia said vehemently.

Boyd took her arm and lifted her out of her chair. "You're right. Let's go. Maybe that coffee shop located another piece of apple pie."

"Apple pie won't help the way I feel tonight. We've got a wonderful chocolate fudge cake at home that Mom made."

Boyd grinned. "A fellow chocoholic, I see. Lead me to that chocolate fudge cake!"

The Lamborghini sprang away from the curb with a muffled roar. Traffic was light, and they arrived quickly at Mia's house. It was a neat white stucco bungalow with a red tile roof. A trellis of maroon bougainvillea added a splash of color to the exterior. There was a square plot of lawn in front and a big olive tree.

Boyd noticed with his practiced eye that the lawn was well tended, the paint fresh and gleaming, and that everything seemed in good repair.

"It's a pretty house," he said. "Have you lived here long?"

"Practically all my life. Dad was a schoolteacher, so we never lived in grand style, but we've always been very happy in this house. I cut the grass every Saturday morning, and Mom does the weeding. We hire somebody for the outside painting, but we paint the rooms ourselves."

Boyd smiled. "Two very self-sufficient women."

"I think female helplessness went out of style with bustles and crinolines." Mia said as she unlocked the front door. "Here, I'll give you a quick tour."

Boyd nodded with approval as they passed through the hall, where family photographs hung, into the slightly formal living room, the cozy family room, and finally the kitchen, which was a cheerful room with green plants and bright daffodil-yellow walls. Nothing in the house looked expensive, but everything was tastefully arranged and furnished.

Mia waved her hand at a chair. "Sit down, while I start the coffee. I make a good cup of coffee, if I do say so myself. I buy the best beans, grind them myself, and use bottled mountain spring water."

In spite of Mia's invitation Boyd had remained standing. "Sounds good. Can I help?"

"Lift the cover off that cake box. You'll see the remains of the most delicious chocolate fudge cake ever made. Cut two big pieces and put them on plates, and we'll have a feast."

A few minutes later the rich aroma of coffee filled the kitchen and mingled with the heavier perfume of chocolate and mocha.

Boyd wrinkled his nose. "I could stand here and just sniff all night long."

Mia laughed. "It's pretty heady stuff, isn't it?" She loaded a tray with a white china pot of coffee, a small creamer and sugar bowl, cups, and the plates of cake. "We're going to consume this in the family room."

Boyd took the tray and followed her. The room was cozy, with paneled walls and comfortable chintz-covered furniture. It also held a piano and stereo equipment.

"Do you like New Age music?" Mia asked. "I've got some great tapes."

Boyd's lips crinkled up in a smile. "New Age would certainly be a change from our problems with old age. Let's listen to your tapes." He ran his gaze down Mia's library of records, CD's, and tapes. "Looks as though you like all kinds of music—classical, opera, rock, jazz."

Mia inserted a tape in the machine. "What I play depends on my mood."

As she straightened, Boyd came up behind her. Encircling her waist with his arms, he pressed his lips to her neck. Mia stood perfectly still, unwilling to break the spell of his delicious kiss or the feel of his hands high under her breasts.

"And what mood are you in tonight, Mia?" he asked. "What do you want to play?"

Mia grasped his hands and pushed them away from her. She took a step toward the coffee table where Boyd had set the tray. "I'm in the mood for coffee and cake," she said with a little laugh.

She seated herself on the soft, oversized couch and poured coffee into each of their cups. Boyd sat down beside her.

"Cream? Sugar?" she asked.

Boyd sniffed at the coffee. "This stuff's too good to be adulterated with anything."

"Wait till you taste the cake."

Boyd took a bite of cake, then put his fork down. "That is absolutely the best chocolate fudge cake I've ever had." He looked deep into her eyes, a mischievous grin lurking at the corners of his mouth. "If you can cook like your mother, I'll marry you on the spot."

"The answer to your question is no. Mom's an exceptional cook. I tried to interest her in teaching an adult education class in cooking, but her heart and soul are in comedy," Mia said and sighed.

"I tried to interest Dad in bingo. You can imagine the results."

"It's as if we're the parents of rebellious teenagers," Mia complained.

"I'll just have to take the motorcycle away from Sonny," Boyd said with mock seriousness.

"And I'll have to insist that Julia stay home nights."

They exploded into laughter.

As they laughed together, Boyd felt a surge of happiness. The feeling grew as he looked at the rosy flush Mia's laughter put on her cheeks and the way her big gray eyes narrowed between her sooty lashes.

Suddenly he wanted to be emotionally close to Mia. She attracted and fascinated him so. He wanted her to know all about him. He felt an irresistible urge to open himself up to Mia, to tell her about Jeanne.

"I was almost married once," Boyd said. "I guess it's just as well we didn't go through with it. If I can't handle my own dad, I don't know how I would have done as a father."

Mia was struck by the novelty of the idea. "That's something I never thought of."

"Her name was Jeanne. We lived together for a year, and we talked about marriage. Then she left me."

Mia arched one eyebrow in a question.

"She went back to her ex-husband. She said he needed her more than I did."

"She was the kind of woman who needs to be needed," Mia murmured.

"That was it exactly. At the time I was pretty torn up, but later I decided it was probably for the best. I believe in an equal partnership between a husband

and wife. One person shouldn't be overly dependent on the other."

Mia nodded. She agreed completely. It was the kind of marriage her mother and father had enjoyed, and theirs had been a very loving, successful one.

She watched Boyd as he took a sip of coffee and ate more cake. In profile his features were strong and clear-cut, his mouth decisive but with a humorous tilt at the corners.

It occurred to her that only a strong man could have made the admission that he had been dumped by the woman he'd loved. Gary couldn't have. Gary was fun-loving like Boyd, but he had a touchy pride, a certain defensiveness about his personality that Boyd lacked completely.

She felt the need to return Boyd's frankness, to be as open with him as he had been with her.

"Relationships can take strange turns," Mia said thoughtfully. "My fiancé, a man I had known for two years and whom I thought I knew very well, left me at the altar on our wedding day."

Boyd let out a whistle of surprise. "Did he ever say why?"

"I never saw or heard from him again. He left town immediately afterward."

"Was it a big wedding?"

"A hundred guests. We've lived in San Ramon all our lives and have a lot of friends as well as relatives. There were also bridesmaids and ushers and me in a white dress—the works. Everything but the groom."

Mia's voice was light, self-mocking. Boyd shot her

a quick, scrutinizing glance. But her limpid gray eyes held no hint of bitterness or pain.

"He was probably a commitmentphobiac," Boyd said. "Commitmentphobia's not that unusual. I've heard of guys calling off their wedding twice. They just panicked and couldn't go through with it."

The dimple showed in Mia's right cheek. "It's rather funny, when you think of it. All these men getting cold feet at the last minute. I can just see them pacing their rooms, trying to decide, should I or shouldn't I?"

Boyd laughed. "Like a horse that comes right up to a hedge, then shies away from jumping over it."

"They're probably waiting for the wrong girl to come along."

"Or a marriage license that expires every few years like a driver's license."

They burst into laughter, facing each other, sharing the joke. When the laughter finally died away, Boyd's eyes grew tender and passionate. He put one arm around Mia's shoulder and encircled her waist with the other. He turned her around and pulled her back until she was reclining in his arms, lying nestled across his hard thighs.

Waiting for his kiss as his lips descended to hers seemed to be the most excitingly agonizing thing Mia had ever done. She had to close her eyes against the ecstasy of it, fraught with breathless anticipation.

Her mouth joined his for a long, thrilling moment. It was as if he had to claim her as his own. Then she felt the hint of his teeth as he nibbled gently at her lower lip.

When he outlined the shape of her mouth with the tip of his tongue, shivers of fiery excitement shot through her. She reached up and wound her arms around his neck, forcing his mouth hard against hers. His tongue plunged aggressively, seeking out and engaging hers in a duel she couldn't escape, didn't want to escape.

The music swelled through the room. Its orchestral tones created pictures for Mia of a night-dark ocean, the moon huge and golden in the sky, pulling on the earth, drawing the waves away from the beach and hurling them forward, over and over again in a cadence as old as time.

The primeval beat loosened something in her, some last caution against love. She wanted him—handsome, sexy, laughter-loving Boyd Baxter—in a way she had never known before. Her breasts strained against the silk of her low-cut dress. She moved restlessly, aware of the tautness of his thighs, of his need, as great as her own.

"I can't get enough of you," Boyd murmured huskily as he began to feather her delicate, vulnerable places with kisses—the fringes of her lashes, the little spot behind her ear, the pulse beating in her throat. Each soft drifting of his lips across her skin fed the whirlpool of her desire.

When he slid his hand inside the plunging neckline of her dress, Mia didn't protest. A soft moan escaped from her as he found the curve of her high, rounded breast.

"You fill my hand perfectly," he said thickly. His thumb stroked the tip of one nipple, bringing it forth until it sprang eagerly into his hand.

In a frenzy to touch him, Mia undid the top button of his open-necked shirt. The second button was harder because she was distracted by the exciting way he was squeezing her breast. When she got it undone, she plunged her hand inside and breathed a tremendous sigh of satisfaction as she felt the soft cloud of curly hair on his chest.

She was deeply aroused, Boyd thought, and not just physically. He could sense her feeling of emotional closeness. They had opened themselves up to each other. They had laughed together and enjoyed the warmth of shared humor.

Instinct told him it wasn't a good idea to make love to Mia now, but he was aching, the blood throbbing through his veins, surging into his groin. He wanted her so badly, he could hardly hold out against the force of his feelings, the demand of his body. What made it worse was the message in her shining gray eyes, in the warm, tender smile on her lips. If he wanted her, that message seemed to read, she was his.

But as his mind thought beyond his painful physical desire for her, beyond the lighthearted sexual pleasure he was used to having with willing partners, beyond the special feelings he had for Mia, Boyd knew that it wasn't the right time. Knowing Mia, he guessed she'd be unhappy with herself and with him in the morning. Then his chance to show her how deeply he cared for her, how much he wanted to be with her—not just for this night but perhaps for always—would be gone.

Boyd eased her up off his lap. "I think I'd better go, Mia, before we do something we regret."

Mia was baffled by Boyd's sudden retreat. She was still trembling from the desire he had aroused in her. Looking for a way to hide her distress, she touched the coffee pot. "The coffee's still hot. Would you like a cup before you leave?"

Her voice was cool and controlled, but there was a slight tremor in it.

"Look, Mia," Boyd said roughly. "This is as hard on me as it is on you. I've never wanted a woman more than I want you tonight. But you're special to me. I think we should wait."

Mia studied him. She noticed the strain of repressed passion on his ruggedly handsome face, the sincerity in his brilliant blue eyes. A thrill went through her, replacing her own unsatisfied desire. Boyd was right, she thought. Going to bed together now would put a stamp on the lovely, still fragile feelings building between them. It would stereotype it in some way, making it conform to a pattern that didn't represent the precious individuality of their relationship.

Mia smiled at Boyd. "I think you're right."

Boyd stood up. "I'd better go now. I'll call you tomorrow."

Mia saw him to the door. They didn't kiss. Their emotions were running too high.

After Boyd left, Mia rewound the tape and removed it from the tapedeck. Then she dumped the coffee down the sink and rinsed off the dishes.

She felt pleasantly excited, full of questions about what would happen between Boyd and her. She knew commitment wasn't the only factor to consider. Once a man and a woman came together, there seemed to be as many possibilities as there were moves on a chessboard. It was just too early in their relationship to tell how it would all turn out.

Mia went to bed and deliberately put her speculations out of her mind so she could sleep. She was awakened by the thrumming of a motor outside on the street. She turned on the light and looked at her clock. It was two A.M.

She heard her mother's high-pitched laughter and Romney's deeper chuckles. They sounded completely in harmony with each other, happy in a relationship that fused friendship with romance and fun.

Mia turned out the light and slid down under the covers. Maybe old age was the best time for love, she thought wistfully. It seemed to be all enjoyment then, no doubts or questions.

The she giggled. She could just see Boyd's face if she suggested that they hold off until they were in their sixties!

Four

"It's for you," Frances said, handing the phone to Mia. She raised her eyebrows and widened her raisin-brown eyes. "He wants to know if the library has a book on how to build an igloo." As Mia took the phone from her, Frances explained, "I told him he'd have to ask the librarian."

"This is Miss Taylor, the librarian," Mia said into the phone. "I'm sure we can help you with your question about igloos."

"That's great. I've got a lot of ice cubes here, and I don't want them to go to waste."

Mia laughed, and the low, infectious music of her voice rang through the library. Browsers and readers looked up from their books and smiled. "Oh, Boyd, you really had me fooled for a minute."

"Listen," Boyd said, "I have a wonderful idea for getting the parents off the garden path and back on the straight and narrow."

"I'm all ears. What is it?"

"I read in the morning paper about a walking group in town that goes on evening walks in various neighborhoods. There's no charge, and anyone's free to join the group. It's healthy exercise in the fresh air. I think our parents would enjoy it, and maybe they'd be too tired after a couple of hours of walking even to think of the comedy club."

"Sounds like a good idea," Mia said. "Particularly as walking is supposed to be good for the heart. Do you think they'll want to do it?"

"I'm sure of it—if we go. Dad said he and Julia wanted to spend more time with us. We'll be a walking foursome, starting tonight. Wear comfortable shoes and bring a flashlight."

"Bring a flashlight *where*, Boyd?"

"Out to my car. I'll pick you up at six-thirty."

Mia hesitated. "It's awfully short notice."

"Then don't bring a flashlight. I'll bring mine."

"Very funny. Where is this walk supposed to take place?"

"I can't tell you. It's the mystery walk of the week."

"Do Julia and Romney know?"

"Romney does. They're going to meet us there at seven."

As she thought about the evening ahead, Mia's lips turned upward in a smile. She was going to see Boyd!

"I think that's a wonderful idea, Boyd. It'll be so good for our parents. I'll be glad to do it for their sakes."

Boyd caught the lilt in her voice and grinned. He couldn't help teasing her a little. "Very noble of you, Mia."

"I can't help it," she said. "It's being surrounded

by books all day. It induces a state of high-minded-ness."

She wasn't very high-minded last night, Boyd thought, his clear blue eyes sparkling with amusement.

"See you at six-thirty," he said, and hung up.

Still wrapped in the deep purr of Boyd's voice, Mia stood looking down at the phone, musing.

"Did you answer that igloo question?" Frances asked.

Mia looked up dreamily. "Igloo? Oh, sure, you build them out of ice cubes."

The January night was clear and warm, even for southern California. Mia wore wheat-colored denim jeans that were pleated at the waist and tapered to the ankle. Over the jeans she had on a sky-blue sweater with one huge wooden button at the throat. She had applied her makeup expertly so that the deep gray of her eyes was accentuated by dark eyeliner and mascara.

She carried an extra sweater just in case and flourished a pencil-slim flashlight at Boyd as he stood at the door of the Lamborghini and held it open for her.

"You're the best-looking footprintmaker I've seen in a long time," Boyd said, raking her from top to bottom with his penetrating gaze.

Mia was pleased with the result she had achieved. Boyd's long glance, full of appreciative admiration, made her thrillingly conscious of her own femininity.

"You don't look exactly like Bigfoot yourself, Boyd," she answered gaily.

On the contrary, Mia thought, he looked incredibly sexy in well-fitting black corduroy slacks and a black cable-knit sweater. When he took the wheel of the car, he looked dashing.

"Do we get to eat on this little jaunt?" Mia asked wistfully. "I didn't have time for supper." She didn't tell him that it was because she was curling her hair, ironing her jeans, and choosing a perfume.

"I understand we'll stop for ice cream afterward."

Mia nodded happily. Ice cream was one of her favorite foods.

As they headed west toward the ocean, she asked, "Are we going to walk on the beach?"

"Just wait, you'll find out," Boyd answered smugly.

"Oh you, you're impossible," Mia said, smiling.

Boyd's arm went around her waist, and he pulled her close to him. "This car likes friendly women."

"How many has it known?" Mia asked.

Boyd turned and looked directly at her. "None as lovely as you."

"Please, Boyd," Mia exclaimed, "keep your eyes on the road."

As they drove through heavy rush-hour traffic, Boyd had to shift gears frequently, and Mia was mesmerized by the movements of his strong hand. She wished she were wearing silk stockings to enhance the exquisite pleasure of his touch when his hand brushed her leg.

Even before Boyd stopped the car, Mia spotted the group. About fifteen people of varying ages, all carrying flashlights, stood on a sidewalk separating a sandy beach from cottages that curved in a crescent along the walk.

Mia looked for Romney's motorcycle. It wasn't there,

but Romney's white head stood out above the crowd, and right beside him was Julia, talking vivaciously and handing out sheets of paper.

Watching her, Mia felt a rush of love. No one could say her mother didn't seize life and enjoy it. Mia could tell she was going to get the most out of their little adventure.

Mia admitted that she, too, felt excited about the evening. She and Boyd would be sharing a new experience together. Someone had once said that love was not a matter of looking into each other's eyes, but of looking out at the world together. It didn't even have to be *love*, Mia told herself. The same philosophy could be applied to a friendly romantic relationship such as she and Boyd were enjoying.

Mia greeted her mother, smiled at the people standing close by, and looked down at the fliers Julia had just given them. She recognized the Laff-A-Minute logo immediately, Underneath was an invitation to spend a laughter-filled evening with fellow walker Julia Taylor at the club.

Mia nudged Boyd. "Look at those leaflets. I don't think your idea is going to work."

"It'll work," Boyd answered confidently. "This is supposed to be a two-hour walk. They'll be so tired at the end of it, all they'll want to do is go home and go to bed."

Boyd took Mia's hand and tucked it in the crook of his arm.

Mia loved feeling the ripple of Boyd's muscles under his sweater. She left her hand where he had placed it. It might make for awkward walking, but the warm tingle that ran through her body was wonderful compensation.

A tall, lanky youth, Mia guessed he was a college student, had joined the group.

"Okay, everybody," he called out. "I'm Jim Gates and I'm to be your leader tonight. First of all, let's introduce ourselves. This is a friendly group, so sing out your names."

When the introductions were over, Jim held up a sheaf of papers. "I've got maps of our itinerary. We're going along Crescent Walk—that's where we are now—to its end, then return by way of the beach. Any questions?" he asked as he passed the maps out.

"Are we stopping for ice cream afterward?" a short, rotund woman asked.

"Absolutely. There's a great little place called Farley's just two streets away where they make their own ice cream."

An "ooh" went up from the crowd.

"Okay," Jim continued. "We're going to start now. It's a two-hour walk. We'll stick together all the way, but if some of you want to do extra sprinting at the end, we'll meet you at Farley's. It's marked on your maps." Jim raised his voice as the group started to move away from the gathering point. "And don't forget to use your flashlights to help yourselves and others. Call out potholes, cracks, rough spots, puddles, dog doo." People laughed. "You get the picture."

Boyd squeezed Mia's hand. "I think this might be fun."

"I just love the idea of people walking together. I also like to explore new territory, and I've never been in this part of town before. Let's find Julia and Romney and walk with them."

Romney's deep voice boomed out. "We're right behind you kids. Good evening, Mia. You're looking particularly lovely tonight."

"Thank you." She slipped her hand out of Boyd's arm. "I think I should walk with the man who pays me compliments, don't you?"

Romney put his arm out. "Take my arm, Mia, and we'll do the Crescent Walk together."

Julia laughed as she and Mia changed places. "It looks as though you're stuck with me, Boyd."

"*Stuck* isn't the right word, Julia. *Honored* is more like it. We'll tell each other jokes to while away the time."

As they walked along, calls of "Puddle!" or "Pothole!" rang out from Jim and the other people in front.

Mia's attention kept drifting to the beach. The outgoing tide lapped at the sand gently. There was a tranquil peace about the evening that she liked. She looked at Boyd talking animatedly with her mother and thought how easy and uncomplicated it was, the four of them out together for a good time.

She turned to Romney, who was beginning to huff and puff a bit beside her. "I didn't see your motorcycle. How did you and Julia get here?"

"Used the car."

"Oh? I thought you two loved the motorcycle and went everywhere on it."

"Sold it."

Mia was too amazed to speak for a moment. The motorcycle was Julia and Romney's symbol of youth, Romney's badge of honor, their pride and joy.

Fear tightened her voice. "Did you have an accident?" They were both obviously in good shape, but some injuries didn't show up until later.

"Nope. I just decided to sell the thing. Didn't like it anymore. A car is much more comfortable."

Romney didn't seem disposed to say any more on the subject, and Mia noticed that he was quite short of breath. Julia was lagging a little behind the others too.

"Time to switch partners," Mia called out gaily. She walked forward and caught up with Boyd, while Julia turned around and rejoined Romney. "Your dad's getting tired," Mia whispered to Boyd.

"He gets a little short-winded when he walks too fast. He'll be all right. I understand the slower walkers usually fall to the rear, then the people in front wait for them to catch up."

"They're both so active, I wouldn't have thought they'd have any trouble with a walk such as this."

"They're probably out of practice," Boyd said wryly. "How much walking have they done lately? They've been tearing around town on his motorcycle."

"Not anymore. Your dad sold it."

As they passed under a streetlight, Mia glanced up into Boyd's handsome, sun-bronzed face. Oddly enough, he didn't look surprised.

"Well, I'm glad he finally came to his senses. Now if we can just get them away from the Laff-A-Minute and keep them out of the Zebra Lounge, we'll have two healthy parents with many years still ahead of them."

Mia didn't answer. Why would Romney sell the motorcycle he was so crazy about? It didn't make sense. And why hadn't Boyd been surprised to hear that he had?

"Look over there," Boyd suddenly said, drawing Mia close to him. "Some people have built fires on the beach."

The sky was black velvet. A fringe of lacy white showed at the water's edge. The beach was dark except for the dancing flames that illumined small areas.

There was something mysterious about the fires, Mia thought. They reminded her of ancient rituals, bonfire signals, messages sent from hill to hill, magical incantations.

She shivered a little and Boyd tightened his grasp on her waist. "Cold, darling?"

"No. Just affected by the scene. It's beautiful and a little eerie at the same time."

"I know what you mean. Years ago in Europe people used to build bonfires at certain times of the year and leap over them to see who would be next to be married. If you could do it without singeing your clothes, you were on your way to the altar. Presumably if you burned your clothes, you'd have nothing to go to the altar in." He glanced teasingly at Mia. "Want to try it?"

Mia shook her head and laughed. "I'd probably end up falling into the fire. I *am* looking forward to the beach part of the walk, however. I love being on the beach at night."

"We can leave now if you like."

"Jim said to stay together."

"We're adults," Boyd pointed out. "I'll just tell him we're splitting and will meet the group at Farley's"

"Okay," Mia said enthusiastically. "I'll run back and let Julia and Romney know."

Mia threaded her way through the other walkers, smiling and excusing herself as she went. When she saw Julia and Romney, she stopped short, enchanted by the sight. They were walking alone, several feet behind the last of the group, but not, Mia thought, because they were still tired.

They had linked arms. Julia had turned to Romney and, laying her other hand on his arm, was looking up into his face with affection. Romney put his hand on Julia's and smiled down at her with an expression of love that made Mia catch her breath.

"Excuse me," Mia called out. "But I just ran back to tell you that Boyd and I are going to start walking on the beach now. We'll meet you at Farley's."

Julia turned to her with dreamy eyes. "That's just fine, dear. Thanks for telling us."

"Do you have your map?" Romney asked.

"Yes." Mia caught herself just in time. She had almost said "Yes, Dad."

By the time she got to the front of the now straggling column, Jim had called a halt to let the slower walkers catch up.

"Boyd and Mia are leaving us at this point to walk on the beach," Jim announced. "They'll meet us at Farley's. Would anyone like to join them?"

Mia caught Boyd's quick frown of dismay. She crossed her fingers and prayed no one would say yes. They were all very pleasant people, but a group walk on the beach was not what she had been looking forward to.

The woman who had asked about stopping for ice cream spoke up. "I think"—Mia held her breath—"I should warn you, sometimes bad elements come to the beach at night."

"She's right," Boyd said. "That's why it's always best to stay with the group."

With that, he took Mia's hand and started for the stairs that led down to the beach.

"How about you?" someone called out.

"We'll outrun the bad elements," Boyd called back over his shoulder.

Mia heard Julia's rather high-pitched laugh and the deep bass of Romney's chuckle as she and Boyd reached the sand.

"Let's take our socks and shoes off." Boyd, with his deep voice, made the suggestion sound more like "Let's take all our clothes off."

They say down side by side on the edge of the walk. In the dim light of a distant lamppost, Mia fumbled with the laces of her running shoes.

"Here, I'll do it for you," Boyd said. He knelt in the sand and quickly unlaced each shoe. He drew of one thick cotton sock but didn't reach for the other one. Instead he cradled her foot in his hand. "It's such a pretty foot. How come you hide it in thick socks and heavy shoes? Why haven't you ever let me see it before?"

Mia laughed and tried to free it from his grasp.

"Unfoot me, you villain," she said dramatically.

Boyd closed his long supple fingers over her foot holding it firmly in his grasp. "Nay, nay, fair lady, cannot give up the loveliest foot in the kingdom."

Mia giggled again. "You sound like a horse, Boyd with that 'nay, nay' business."

"Don't distract me. I have other things in mind."

Mia had always heard that the foot was one of the most sensitive parts of the anatomy but hadn't believed it until now. Just the touch of Boyd's strong fingers under her arch sent tremors of excitement through her.

He bent his head and slowly laid a trail of kisses along her instep. The pressure of his warm, moist mouth on her sensitive skin was electrifying. She had to hold on to something to contain the thrill she felt. She leaned back and put her hands behind her on the concrete.

"A knight always plays fair," Boyd said wickedly. Mia wondered what he meant until he pulled off her other shoe and sock. Waiting and wondering what he would do put her in a fever of anticipation.

Slowly he closed his lips over each straight pink toe and kissed it.

Every soft little tug at her toes was matched by a demanding pulsing deep inside her. She closed her eyes to savor each new and wonderful sensation sweeping through her. A purr of pleasure escaped from her throat and was borne away on the velvety night air.

The clink of a beer can as it hit a nearby wire mesh trash container broke into the night's peace. Rough-sounding male voices drew closer.

"Let's go," Boyd whispered.

They picked up their socks and shoes and walked through the thick sand until they reached the water's edge.

"Ooh, it's cold," Mia exclaimed as the water washed over her ankles.

"It's good for you. It'll cool you down," Boyd said mischievously.

"And just how cold do you want me?"

Boyd laughed and threw his hands up in the air. "You win. I surrender. But watch where you put your feet, you don't want to step on a sharp shell."

"There are plenty of beach fires tonight. I think I can see well enough."

But a minute later something cold and wet and

slimy had wrapped itself around her ankle. She tried to step away from it, and her foot landed on a small, squishy nodule. The image of the eight writhing arms of an octopus with their rows of sucker disks flashed through Mia's mind. Her scream was broken as she tripped and started to fall.

Boyd caught her as she started to go down. "It's only a big piece of kelp, darling. Hold still, I'll get it off."

She shivered in his arms. "Quickly, please, Boyd. It feels horrible."

"It's because you can't see it." He flicked on his flashlight and adroitly freed her foot from the long strand of seaweed.

Mia laughed nervously. "I thought it was an octopus."

"An octopus out of water? On the beach?"

"I didn't stop to analyze," Mia said.

They picked up their socks and shoes and resumed their walk, moving up the sand to be closer to the beach fires. They stopped from time to time to chat with people who waved or called out hellos.

Every time they did so, Boyd kept his arm loosely around Mia's waist in a possessive gesture. It gave Mia a warm, protected feeling as they met other couples or families. Sometimes children who were toasting marshmallows over the fire would solemnly hold one out, black and dripping, at the end of a stick for Mia or Boyd to take.

When they reached the stairs at the opposite end of the beach, Boyd said lightly, "This is where we get off." He squeezed her waist. "It was nice, wasn't it?"

"Umm," Mia answered, the remains of a marshmallow in her mouth.

Boyd turned on his flashlight. "Hey, you're a marsh-mallow mess, you know that?"

He drew her into the shadows. He nibbled gently at her lower lip where a bit of marshmallow had stuck. When he'd removed it, he licked the sticky corners of her mouth.

"Let's see if I got you clean," he said huskily. He took her face between his hands and held it still for a long breath-quickening kiss. Then his tongue surged between her lips, demanding the warmth beyond, and he moved his mouth on hers in a slow, darkly sensuous dance of love.

With his hands flat against her waist, he urged her closer and Mia went unthinkingly. She raised her arms to encircle his neck, and he pulled her more tightly against the hard leanness of his body.

"We're a perfect fit, darling," Boyd said. "Let me show you." He passed his hands with tantalizing slowness over the length of her back from the nape of her neck to her hips, melding her intimately against him every inch of the way. He curved his fingers into her rounded bottom and pressed her closer. His manhood surged against her, and she thrilled at the effect she had on him.

Then common sense reasserted itself. She slid her hands down his chest. "We have to get back to the group. We promised."

He released her with a tremendous sigh. "All right. Let's go."

They walked into Farley's to a chorus of "Well, there they are!" and "At last!" and "We were worried about you."

Mia became a little flustered. She smiled and grew pink. She turned to Boyd to see how he was taking the group's interest in them, but he didn't seem to be paying attention. There was a thoughtful, tender look on his face. Mia followed the direction of his gaze.

Romney and Julia were sitting alone at a small round marble-topped table in the rear of the room. Mia didn't think they had even noticed that she and Boyd had arrived. Each of them had a double-dip ice-cream cone. Julia's was a tiered pink strawberry mountain; Romney's was two-toned—chocolate and vanilla.

Laughing, they joined arms across the table and took licks from each other's cones.

"That must be what they did when they were young," Boyd said, a wistful tone in his voice. "It must have been nice then. People stayed married, families stayed in one place, kids read books instead of watching the boob tube."

"Don't forget the depression, unemployment without anything to cushion the blow, and the Second World War," Mia added gently.

Boyd draped his arm around her shoulders. "You're right," he said humorously. "We always forget the downside in nostalgia."

They sauntered over to Romney and Julia's table and sat down.

"How was your walk?" Mia asked.

"Lovely, just lovely." Julia sighed. "Weren't the beach fires pretty?"

Romney looked meaningfully at Julia. "Maybe we'll do this again, since we don't have the motorcycle anymore."

"Walking is certainly a lot safer," Boyd said. He got to his feet and looked down into Mia's face. "What will you have?"

You, she thought. She wanted him very, very badly. He could have taken her last night or even just now on the beach. She was lovestruck, moonstruck, spellbound. And she just didn't know where it was all going to lead.

"A double vanilla cone," she told Boyd.

Julia looked at her, surprised. "But you don't like vanilla. You never eat it."

"I'm going to tonight." Vanilla, which she absolutely loathed, would be her punishment, her just dessert for always yielding to Boyd's kisses. "Are you going home after this, Mom?" Mia asked.

"Oh no, I'm going to perform at the Laff-A-Minute." Julia waved her hand around the room. "I've persuaded most of our new friends to come too."

Well, that's one stratagem that didn't work, Mia thought gloomily.

"Have you written new material for Julia?" she asked Romney.

Oddly enough it was Julia who answered. "Yes, he has, and it's absolutely marvelous. Romney's really hitting his stride now."

"That's great," Mia said absently. She looked directly at Romney. "I'm awfully glad you got rid of that motorcycle. Boyd and I were really worried about your safety."

"Not having the motorcycle to tear around on will give me more time to work on Julia's material. A motorcycle for jokes seems like a fair exchange to me."

Julia's face turned the color of her strawberry ice cream.

When Boyd returned with a double-scoop of plain vanilla for Mia and a luscious butterpecan and fudgeripple combo for himself, Mia looked at him speculatively.

Jokes for a motorcycle. Had Boyd double-crossed her? Had he made a deal with his dad to furnish him with funny jokes in exchange for Romney's selling his beloved motorcycle?

The end result was wonderful. Mia was overjoyed to hear that the motorcycle was gone. Now she wouldn't have to quiver with anxiety at seeing her mother put on the ridiculously oversized helmet, or lie awake nights waiting to hear the familiar *vroom-vroom* outside the house.

But if Boyd made a deal with Romney, why hadn't he told her? Why had he let her believe that he was supplying Julia with *bad* jokes? Didn't he trust her enough to take her into his confidence?

Mia was quiet all the way home. She would have to ask Boyd exactly what he had done, but not now, she thought. It had been a wonderful evening, and Mia hated to spoil the magic of it.

Boyd glanced at her several times, wondering why she was so preoccupied, but he refrained from asking questions. He told himself it was because he respected Mia's privacy, but deep inside he had a sense of foreboding.

Five

When Mia got up the next morning, she found her mother at the kitchen table drinking coffee, a sheaf of typewritten pages in front of her.

Julia shot her a quick, searching glance. A worried look followed. "You don't look very healthy after last night's walk. Do you think you're coming down with something?"

"I didn't sleep well last night."

Julia raised her eyebrows. "Oh? You should have come to the comedy club. A little laughter might have relaxed you. Maybe I should say a *lot* of laughter." She bent her head coyly. "I wish you had been there, Mia. I really got a lot of laughs. In fact, Mr. Baker, the owner, asked me to come back tonight, and he's going to pay me. It's not much—I'm not a headliner yet—but it's a start."

Mia poured herself a cup of coffee. "That's wonderful, Mom. I guess Romney's material improved when he got rid of his motorcycle." She was fishing, but she didn't get a rise out of her mother, just an ambiguous smile before she bent her head to the typewritten pages again.

"Tonight's jokes?" Mia asked.

"Yes. Fresh material." Almost girlishly, Julia asked, "Would you mind checking my delivery?"

"Not at all," Mia answered, reaching for the typewritten sheets.

As Julia ran through her material, Mia had to admit that the routines were very funny. Also, the more she listened, the more the jokes sounded as if Boyd had written them. Personality branded everything a person did; how one drove a car, made love, and joked. And the jokes had Boyd's cleverness and his wry, self-deprecating touch.

Romney's would sound different. Romney's *had* sounded different, Mia remembered.

Recalling Romney's comment and Julia's confusion at Farley's ice-cream shop the previous night, Mia was convinced that Boyd had struck a bargain with his dad. He would write Julia's material if Romney got rid of his motorcycle.

Harboring a grudge or being resentful was not Mia's way, however. She had a forgiving nature, which affected her relationships with everyone, but particularly influenced her feelings for Boyd. They had already been so open with each other, had exchanged so many confidences about themselves and their past disappointments in love that Mia wouldn't consider having anything less than total frankness between them now. As soon as possible, she would ask Boyd exactly what had transpired between him and his dad.

"Well, what do you think?" Julia asked.

"I think the material is great, just great. My compliments to Romney"—she looked Julia straight in the eye—"or whoever."

Julia looked away, unable or unwilling to hold Mia's gaze. "Romney will be coming by soon. We're going to the movies this afternoon."

Mia was concerned. "Don't you think you should rest, Mom?"

"I'll rest when I'm old," Julia said matter-of-factly.

"Right, Mom." Movies, a comedy act, the Zebra Lounge, Mia thought, just your average senior citizen's day.

Mia called Boyd from the library. It was a Saturday, and he was home.

"Hey, my lucky day," Boyd said when he answered the phone. "What do you have in mind?"

"I thought I'd come see your etchings."

"Terrific! I'll run right out and buy some."

Mia laughed, and Boyd listened with delight to the low throaty chuckle that thrilled him every time he heard it. "I thought I'd bring over a casserole and a loaf of French bread."

"This is getting better all the time."

"How about salad makings?"

"At last look inside my refrigerator, I had lettuce, tomatoes, a cucumber, and red onion," he said.

"Sounds good. The library closes at five. Is six-thirty all right with you?"

"The wine will be chilled, the candles lit, the etchings hung. Wear something comfortable. I'm giving the butler the night off."

Mia had a hard time staying under the speed limit

on the way home. The spray was still flying off her when she stepped out of the shower. She wiggled her way into a long-sleeved leotard top in goldenrod-yellow and put on a short black skirt, adding a black patent leather belt with a silver buckle. Makeup on, she grabbed one of Julia's coq au vin casseroles from the freezer and stuck a long loaf of French bread under her arm.

On the road again, Mia felt an exciting sense of anticipation. At a red light she slid several silver bracelets onto her wrist and inserted a pair of silver hoop earrings in her ear lobes. She checked her appearance in the rearview mirror, dabbed some perfume behind her ears, tapped her fingers to the music on the car radio, and smiled happily—her thoughts on the evening ahead.

She could picture the scene. The table would be beautifully set, soft music would fill the room, she'd share a delicious supper with Boyd. They would joke and tease each other a little, maybe talk seriously about themselves, exchange more confidences. From time to time there would be long, comfortable pauses —proof of how at ease they were with each other.

By the time she pulled up to the elegant condominium building, Mia had almost forgotten she intended to ask Boyd some searching questions.

When Boyd opened the door to her, Mia caught her breath. He looked unbelievably handsome and sexy, his chestnut hair tightly curled and still damp from the shower, his broad shoulders stretching the cable stitches of a white V-neck sweater, his slim hips accentuated in mahogany-brown cords.

He took the flowered casserole dish from her hands. "Smells good."

"It can't. It's still frozen."

"I meant you." He leaned forward and kissed her lightly on the lips. "Come in and see what I've done. I've surpassed even my own wildest expectations."

Mia gasped as she followed him into the living room. The scene was just as she had pictured it. The table was set in the dining alcove with a pristine white cloth, flowers, and fine china and crystal. Soft, melodic music poured from the stereo speakers. Through the big picture window, the harbor lights twinkled prettily in the softly falling darkness.

"It's beautiful, Boyd. Where did you learn to do things so nicely?"

Boyd led the way into the kitchen. "Mom believed boys should help with the dishes and so forth. If I had had a sister, I'm sure Dad would have taught her auto mechanics. My parents really believed in equality between the sexes."

"I think mine did, too, except that I was only twelve when my dad died, so I grew up closer to my mom." Mia paused thoughtfully. "As you did with your dad after your mother's death."

They studied each other, searching for answers.

"Do you think we're being overprotective of Julia and Romney?" Boyd asked. "After all, they *are* adults, and they've had more life experience than we've had. They're both successful people, too, which shows that they have good judgment."

"Or *had* good judgement," Mia said. "I think what's happening to them could happen to people at any age. They're doing what they want to do regardless of the consequences. They're being carried along by their desire to capture their youth or be successful or just have fun, like wood chips in a stream."

Boyd nodded vigorously. "I think you're right. When the people you love stop thinking wisely for themselves, then it's time to step in and help them."

He slid the casserole into the oven and took the bread from Mia. Putting it on the chopping board, he started to slice it.

"Isn't there something you'd like me to do?" Mia asked.

"I saved a job for you. You can throw croutons in the salad. At the very last minute we'll toss it with the salad dressing. It'll be a while before your casserole gets heated through. Would you like a glass of wine."

"Yes, please."

As she sipped the wine, Mia watched Boyd's large, graceful hands slice the bread with deft strokes. For a big man all his movements were competent and even elegant in their efficiency.

He turned to her suddenly. Mia was embarrassed. He must have caught her look of admiration. "A penny for your thoughts," he said, his vibrant blue eyes reflecting back to her the lustrous gleam in her own gray ones.

Before she could stop herself, the words slipped out. "You're beautiful."

"Mia!" he said huskily. He pulled her close to him and bent his head to kiss her. The strength of his arms as he wrapped them around her, the clean, virile scent of soap and after-shave, the touch of his lips on hers were agonizing, because they made her want him so. But there was still the important question she had to ask. So, difficult as it was, she kept her body rigid, her lips closed.

Laughing, Boyd released her. "I think you're hungry. Supper's ready. C'mon and do your thing with the croutons. Then we'll eat."

When should she ask him about Julia's material? she wondered. As she put the finishing touches on the salad, Mia pondered her dilemma. The best time was now, she decided. She'd get it over with before dinner.

On the other hand she was hungry and the smell of the casserole Boyd had just pulled out of the oven was tempting. Maybe after dinner would be better.

Lost in thought, Mia thrust her hand into the box of flavored croutons and scattered them over the salad. Then she plunged her hand into the crouton box again and threw her catch onto the salad.

"Hey, Mia, don't take your job so seriously. There's more bread than lettuce in that salad." He bent down and looked into her face. "But don't feel bad, honey. I like croutons. I'd use them all the time, except that they're hard to make a sandwich with."

He started to put his finger under her chin to lift it. She knew a kiss would come next. If he kissed her, she'd never ask him the question that weighed so heavily on her mind. She turned her head abruptly.

"We'd better eat," Boyd said humorously, "or I'm not going to get anywhere with you tonight."

They carried the food to the table and sat down. Boyd lifted his glass of sparkling wine and proposed a toast: "To us and to the evening."

They sipped, their gazes meeting over the rim of the glasses.

"My compliments on the croutons," Boyd said, as he ate his salad. "They're superb. How do you do it? Do you throw a single clump, scatter a handful, or pitch a few at a time?"

To his surprise Mia didn't laugh. Her expression was serious and troubled.

"What's the matter, Mia?" he asked quietly.

"Have you been writing Julia's routines?" she asked, looking him square in the eye. Without her willing it, the question had suddenly surfaced, demanding to be answered.

Boyd was taken aback. It wasn't the question that startled him—he intended to tell Mia sooner or later anyway—but her tone of voice was slightly belligerent, as if he had done something wrong.

"Sure, I've been writing your mom's jokes," Boyd admitted.

"Right from the beginning?" Angry spots of red colored Mia's cheekbones. "From the time you told me you would insert *unfunny* jokes in Romney's material?"

"That's what I fully intended to do," Boyd explained. "But I couldn't carry it through. After I drove you home that night, I sat down and reread the stale old jokes I'd showed you and found I just couldn't write junk like that. You've got to understand, Mia," he pleaded, "I'm used to always doing my best. It hurts me to turn out inferior work of any kind."

Mia bent her head and thoughtfully took a bite of her chicken. She recognized the truth of Boyd's argument. His striving for excellence was intrinsic to his personality. Incompetency in any field, even writing jokes, was impossible for him even to consider.

She appreciated the quality in Boyd. She felt the same way, but the hurt inside her persisted. Why hadn't he told her?

"So I rewrote the jokes I showed you that night,"

Boyd continued. "I added some others and slipped the page into Romney's folder."

"And Romney caught on." It was more a statement than a question.

"Not at first," Boyd said quickly. "But after a while he noticed the difference between his typewriter and mine. So he came to me and asked me about it."

"How did he know you were the one writing the jokes?"

"I'd say it was a logical guess. Anyway," Boyd went on, "Dad could see that my material was getting laughs and his wasn't. He really cares for your mom and wants her to be successful, since her heart is so set on it. So he asked if I would continue writing Julia's material."

"And that's when you made the deal."

"Right," Boyd said, glad that she understood his motive. "I told him I'd write the jokes if he gave up the motorcycle."

Remembering how proud Romney had looked with his helmet tucked under his arm, how eagerly he slipped into the leather saddle, Mia said in a tone tinged with awe, "And he sold his motorcycle!"

"He did it for your mom. I'm sure he wouldn't have given it up for any other reason."

"But why didn't you tell me?" Mia asked.

"I tried to several times, but something always prevented it."

"How about Mom? Does she know?"

"Dad asked me not to tell her. Dad had his male ego to consider. He wants your mom to admire him. She believed he was writing her material, and he wanted her to continue believing it, especially as the jokes were getting laughs."

"I think Mom suspects anyway."

Boyd shrugged and resumed eating.

Mia watched the long lean line of his jaw as he chewed. Again she had the almost irresistible desire to run her finger down the cleft in his chin. Her heart whispered to her to forget her quarrel with him, but her mind insisted on more answers.

"I still think if you had wanted to, you would have told me."

Boyd raised his expressive dark brows. "Maybe I didn't really want to," he admitted. "Maybe I was afraid you'd be mad at me. I knew how much you worried about your mother being in that club all the time, but I figured getting them off the motorcycle was more important than putting an end to Julia's career."

"Oh, it was. I don't deny that. What bothers me is that you didn't trust my judgment enough to tell me what you were doing."

Boyd looked puzzled. "I thought I was doing what we both wanted. Maybe I was a little wrong in trying to protect you from knowing the means I used, but—"

"A *little* wrong!" Mia said in a hurt voice as she rose from the table.

Boyd got up too. He reached her in two strides and planted his hands on the sides of her head, tilting her face up to his. "All right, I'll admit that I was completely wrong, that I should have told you." His voice dropped an octave to a husky purr and his lips slowly approached hers. "Now will you forgive me?"

Mia pursed her lips to say "No!" She wasn't going to trade her honesty for one of his kisses. But Boyd must have taken her puckering up as an invitation.

Before she could utter a sound, he was holding her head steady to receive the full power of his demanding kiss. He took advantage of her breathed protest by sliding his tongue between her lips, then plummeting it deep into her mouth.

She slid her hands upward, meaning to push him away, but somehow she ended up with her arms around his neck. Then she inched her fingers upward into his thick curly hair. She met his tongue boldly, and they drank feverishly of each other, trying to slake their passion.

As Boyd inched closer, pressing her softness against him, warning signals went off in Mia's mind. This was not the scenario she had visualized. When she got up from the table, she had planned a quick march to the door before he could capture her with his sweet, inflaming kisses.

"Boyd!" she said in a breathy voice.

"Yes, darling." He buried his face in her perfumed neck and tried to nibble her ear.

"No, Boyd. I'm leaving. I need time to think about what you told me tonight."

He dropped his hands and held her away from him. "Why can't you just accept my apology and forgive me?"

"I do accept your apology and forgive you. It's my own feelings I want to get in touch with. I need time to think."

His hands dropped to his sides. His brilliant blue eyes shone with a mixture of amusement and concern. "Don't think so hard that you forget to come back," he said softly.

"I won't," Mia replied.

But as she drove home, Mia was seized with a

confusion of feelings: A lingering anger with Boyd, regret that he hadn't been totally honest with her, and an overwhelming desire to clear the whole matter up immediately.

She had to tell Julia who had been writing her material. Honesty went right across the board. If you loved people, you were honest with them.

When Mia got home, Julia was in the kitchen, preparing the next morning's coffee ahead of time. She had her gray hair up in rollers and had already changed into her flower-sprigged flannel nightgown, pink chenille bathrobe, and bunny slippers.

"Isn't it early for you to go to bed, Mom?"

"Mr. Baker asked me to go on again tomorrow night. Romney and I both thought I should get a good night's sleep once in a while."

"Well, that was good advice." Mia stood looking gloomily around the immaculate kitchen. She hated to cause her mother pain by telling her that Romney, the man she loved, was not the author of her comedy routines. But she firmly believed that a person couldn't make sound judgments about other people without knowing all about them. In the long run she'd be doing Julia a favor by telling her.

"Mom, I have something to tell you."

"I thought you did." Julia sighed. "It looks like bad news, so I think I'll take it sitting down."

Julia seated herself at the butcher block kitchen table, and Mia took a chair opposite her.

"Romney hasn't been writing your material—not since it's gotten good, anyway. Boyd has."

"I know that, dear," Julia said placidly.

Mia was dumbfounded. It was the last answer she would have expected. "You knew that? Boyd said

America's most popular, most compelling romance novels...

Here, at last...love stories that really involve you! Fresh, finely crafted novels with story lines so believable you'll feel you're actually living them! Characters you can relate to...exciting places to visit...unexpected plot twists...all in all, exciting romances that satisfy your mind and delight your heart.

EXAMINE 6 LOVESWEPT NOVELS FOR

15 Days FREE!

To introduce you to this fabulous service, you'll get six brand-new Loveswept releases not yet in the bookstores. These six exciting new titles are yours to examine for 15 days without obligation to buy. Keep them if you wish for just $12.50 plus postage and handling and any applicable sales tax.

☐ **YES,** please send me six new romances for a 15-day FREE examination. If I keep them, I will pay just $12.50 (that's six books for the price of five) plus postage and handling and any applicable sales tax and you will enter my name on your preferred customer list to receive all six new Loveswept novels published each month *before* they are released to the bookstores—always on the same 15-day free examination basis.

40311

Name_____

Address_____

City_____

State_____Zip_____

My Guarantee: I am never required to buy any shipment unless I wish. I may preview each shipment for 15 days. If I don't want it, I simply return the shipment within 15 days and owe nothing for it.

R6234

Get one full-length Loveswept FREE every month!
Now you can be sure you'll never, ever miss a single
Loveswept title by enrolling in our special reader's home
delivery service. A service that will bring you all six new
Loveswept romances each month for the price of five—and
deliver them to you before they appear in the bookstores!

Examine 6 Loveswept Novels for

15 days FREE!

(SEE OTHER SIDE FOR DETAILS)

Postage will be paid by addressee

Loveswept

Bantam Books
P.O. Box 985
Hicksville, NY 11802

BUSINESS REPLY MAIL
FIRST-CLASS MAIL   PERMIT NO. 2456   HICKSVILLE, NY

NO POSTAGE
NECESSARY
IF MAILED
IN THE
UNITED STATES

you didn't. Romney doesn't know you do, and you certainly didn't tell me."

Nothing she had said ruffled Julia. She folded her hands in her lap, blinked sleepily at Mia, and said, "There was no need to tell anybody that I knew— certainly not Romney. It would have hurt his pride. He loved writing jokes for me, feeling that we were partners, that it wasn't *my* success but *ours*."

"Didn't Romney notice that the jokes you told weren't his?"

"Oh, I always used a few of his. Then, too, his hearing isn't very good, and he tends to be a bit absentminded. Not because of his age," Julia added hurriedly. "It's all the weighty things on his mind."

"Uh-huh," Mia answered. "So Boyd was fooling me, Romney thought he was fooling you, and you were fooling everybody."

"I was trying to keep Romney happy, dear. Happiness is a rare state, especially in old age, when there's so much sickness and pain. It's worth a few white lies to make someone you love happy."

Mia shook her head. "I don't see it. I just don't see any substitute for honesty in human relationships, *especially* between people who love each other."

"Maybe someday you will, Mia," her mother said softly. "How did you find out that Boyd was writing my material?"

"Romney's remarks in Farley's about exchanging jokes for the motorcycle made me suspicious. How did *you* find out?"

"I was astounded when Romney told me he was going to sell his motorcycle. He just loved that machine." Julia's voice broke a little. "And so did I. Sure, we knew it was dangerous, but it was exciting, too, and it gave us a sense of power to go zooming down the freeway, weaving in and out of traffic."

Mia closed her eyes in horror. The thought of seventy-year-old Romney with her petite mother clutching his waist, darting between cars on a motorcycle was more than she could bear. It took a determined effort not to envision the ambulance drawn up on the side of the road and the white-coated attendants.

"When I kept asking him *why*," Julia went on, "he was so evasive, I began to be suspicious. At the same time there was a definite change for the better in my material. Romney's jokes are improving rapidly, but Boyd's still outshine them in every way."

That's my Boyd, Mia thought proudly. Then she immediately tamped down her reaction. Maybe she should get out of the habit of thinking of Boyd as hers—of thinking of him at all.

"You know, there was only one thing—or, rather, person—Romney loved more than his motorcycle," Mia pointed out.

Julia cast her gaze downward. "I realized that when he sold his beloved motorcycle." When she looked at Mia again, her hazel eyes were shining with happiness. "How could I tell him that I knew he wasn't writing my material, that someone else was writing the jokes that were getting me laughs for the first time in my career?"

"If yours and Romney's love for each other is strong, surely it could withstand the truth, damaging as it might be to Romney's ego."

Julia looked at her daughter skeptically. "*Ego* has a disparaging ring to it. *Pride* sounds better, and *self-respect* even better. Being a successful comedy writer was Romney's way of retaining respect in a society which tends, at best, to be uninterested in the elderly. At worst, old people are treated with patronizing contempt. That's hard for anyone, especially a proud man like Romney, to take."

"I understand, Mom," Mia said sympathetically.

"I'm glad you do. I really am, Mia." Julia yawned and got up from the table. "Well, I'm going to bed. Monday's a holiday, and Laff-A-Minute's expecting a big weekend crowd."

In all her stress and turmoil, Mia had forgotten that the library would be closed on Monday.

She had a sudden urge to be completely alone. It was hard to think as deeply as she wanted. She and her mother owned a cabin in the mountains. It was a simple A-frame painted a cheerful red, set off by itself halfway up a hill in a stand of pines.

Her family used to go there when her father was alive. Mia had held slumber parties there, filling the cabin with screaming, giggling girls. When her mother was teaching, the two of them would use the cabin when they wanted a restful weekend or a longer vacation.

Mia loved the cool air of the mountains, the western lilac that grew there in the spring, the wild flowers that she never saw in the city. The cabin held memories of good times. It also was a refuge. When Gary had jilted her, Mia went to the cabin to be alone with her disappointment and to renew herself through the simple, natural pleasure the mountains gave her.

"I think I'll spend the weekend at the cabin, Mom.

I'll drive up early tomorrow morning and return Monday evening."

Julia studied her daughter's sad, troubled face. "Something happened between you and Boyd." It was a statement not a question.

"We had a little disagreement," Mia answered airily. "That's all."

"I certainly hope it wasn't anything serious. I like Boyd. He's almost as good a man as his father. Good-night, dear."

"Good-night, Mom."

Six

Mia was awakened early in the morning by a branch scraping across her window. The storm the forecaster had predicted arrived during the night, lashing the area with a cold, windy rain. Such severe weather usually meant snow in the mountains, so Mia packed some ski clothes and wore a heavy powder-blue wool sweater under her yellow slicker. She moved quickly, eager to get an early start. Tiptoeing into the kitchen, she left a note for her mother propped up against the coffeepot, and let the car roll silently down the driveway before she put it in gear and drove off.

A feeling of exhilaration seized her as she entered the almost empty freeway and her windshield wipers scooped furiously back and forth across the glass. Although not a loner by nature, Mia felt good about what she was doing. All bridges between her and the people closest to her would be down for the weekend. Alone with herself, she'd be able to sort things out.

It was particularly important that she not see Boyd. She didn't want to be persuaded by his charm, to have her senses overwhelmed by the attraction she felt for him, to have the flickering of love inside herself fanned into a roaring bonfire. A bonfire in which she would singe more than her clothes, Mia thought wryly, recalling Boyd's anecdote about how the ancients foretold marriage.

But as she drove along, seemingly the only person in a watery world, with nothing to focus on but some insipid songs on the car radio, memories came flooding back. The kisses they had exchanged on the beach, the feel of his body as he pressed her tight against him, the glorious, soaring passion that he had ignited within her—all were poignantly fresh in her mind.

What, she asked herself next, was she doing all alone on a rainy highway, hell-bent to nowhere? Wasn't she overreacting to the situation? Going to extremes?

An overwhelming urge to turn around and drive straight to Boyd's condo took hold of her. She pictured him coming to the door. Did he sleep in the nude? Mia's breathing quickened a little at the thought.

He'd be surprised. His vivid blue eyes would open wide, then almost close in a half-amused, half-knowing look.

Maybe he'd say something funny such as "To what do I owe the honor?" or "You look like a little school crossing guard in that yellow slicker." Then he'd put his hand on her arm and lead her in.

Would they have breakfast first or afterward? Mia speculated. Afterward, she decided. It wasn't food they were both hungry for, but each other.

His bed would still be warm from his body. He would undress her slowly, reverently.

Reverently? With a thick woolen ski sweater and a tailored shirt underneath? Mia glanced down at herself in disgust. If she had known what her fantasy was going to be, she would have dressed differently.

Besides, she had overlooked her grievance against him. What would she say when she entered? "I forgive you for deceiving me?"

She *did* forgive him. She wasn't really one to hold a grudge. What she couldn't do was trust him. He had broken his word to her once. There was a good chance he'd do it again. There was no place in her life for men who broke promises. Not anymore. Not after Gary Morgan.

Granted, she realized, there was a huge difference between Gary's offense and Boyd's failure to tell her the truth. But Boyd was the first man she had been strongly attracted to since Gary. Mia found that a small, hard core of fear seemed to have lodged inside her. When she thought of a serious relationship with Boyd, her heart fluttered with apprehension.

A convenient off-ramp for reversing direction came into sight. Mia slowed down, then, on impulse, she pressed her foot against the accelerator and sped past it. There'd be no turning back now, she thought.

Two hours later, when she had almost reached the cabin, Mia stopped at a country store to buy food. Staples like sugar and coffee, cleaning supplies, bedding, and firewood were always left at the cabin, and Mia and Julia usually brought food they had cooked in the city. But food had been the last thing on Mia's mind when she'd left home.

By the time she had assembled all her purchases on the counter, the owner was serving another customer and Mia had to wait. Looking down at what she had bought—one can of beans, a small loaf of bread, one stick of butter, a package of franks, one steak, one baking potato—she was struck by a wave of loneliness.

Mia didn't like to eat alone. She and Frances usually brought their lunches and managed somehow to eat at the same time. Occasionally Mia would go out to the little coffee shop nearby and lunch with a friend.

She felt dismal and blue, which was no way to start a weekend of serious introspection. She'd be climbing the walls if she didn't snap out of it. So to cheer herself up, Mia grabbed a bag of chocolate chip cookies and put them on the counter.

"Will that be all, miss?" the store owner asked, nodding and smiling a good-bye to his previous customer.

As his gaze traveled over her purchases, Mia suddenly felt ashamed. The oneness of everything made her look friendless and unloved.

She grabbed another bag of cookies. "I'm expecting company." She waved her hand vaguely at the other foods. "They're light eaters."

The man nodded politely and rang everything up on the cash register.

It had stopped snowing sometime during the early morning, but as Mia's small car continued to climb the mountain, the fields on both sides of the highway were covered with snow. The road had been cleared and the snow banked on each side, so chains weren't necessary.

The side road up to the cabin was a different story. Mia had to slow down to a crawl to keep the car from sliding on the ice and crashing into one of the pine trees lining the road.

When the cabin came into view, she gave a little gasp of delight. It looked like a scene on a Christmas card—its red frame standing out bright and sharp against the snow-covered dark green pines. All it needed was smoke curling from the chimney, and she was going to see to that right away.

Her spirits restored, Mia bounded out of the car and carried her groceries in. She turned on the wall panel gas heater to take the chill off the cabin, then put the food away in the small refrigerator and knotty pine cupboards. A short while later she had a roaring fire going in the fieldstone fireplace.

Looking around as she unsnapped her yellow slicker, Mia checked the cabin to make sure everything was as it should be. There was always the worry that someone would break in when the place was unoccupied.

The memory of laughter and young voices, of her father's mellow tones and her mother's youthful giggle made the silence of the cabin unbearable. A long walk was what she needed to burn off her loneliness. After that she'd settle into the routine of being alone. It was only for two days, she reminded herself.

Mia turned off the heat and banked the fire. She threw a parka over her ski sweater and set out on a trail that led through the woods. The sun had come up, which meant the snow wouldn't last long, but the radiance of the day and the sparkle of sunshine on the pristine white snow were compensation enough.

Mia's spirits lifted with the beauty of the scene and the pleasure of vigorous exercise. She passed other cabins, some unoccupied, some with smoke weaving up into the blue sky from the chimney, and soon came to a hill where children were coasting on sleds, plastic trash bags, and even big pieces of cardboard.

She was suddenly filled with a longing to go whizzing down the hill with the kids, the dry snow squeaking under the sled runners, the cold wind on her cheeks. Her father had built a long, tobogganlike sled for her and her friends. Mia wondered idly if it was still in the storage shed behind the cabin.

It might look strange—a grown woman coasting down the hill with a lot of little kids. Mia shrugged. She didn't care how she looked. It would be fun.

She turned to go back, glancing at her watch at the same time. Julia would have read her note by now. There wasn't a phone in the cabin, so even if Boyd did ask where she was and Julia told him, Mia wouldn't hear from him.

She couldn't see Boyd risking his precious Lamborghini on the mountain road that led to the cabin. Not only was it icy, but falling rock and tree branches could scrape the car's satiny black finish which Boyd was so proud of.

Suddenly Mia realized that in a secret corner of her mind she had wanted Boyd to follow her. It would be proof that he cared for her. She tried to avoid setting up the opposite scenario: If he didn't come, it meant that he didn't care. A wisp of that idea lingered in her mind, too, but she chased it away with the reminder that it was she, after all, who had left him.

She had been foolish, she realized. The sudden insight pierced her consciousness painfully. She had been projecting Gary's faults onto Boyd. Both men were amusing and fun to be with, but beyond that the similarities ended. Gary, Mia now saw, was emotionally shallow, whereas Boyd had depths of feeling and intellect that matched her own. He was dependable and solid, a person capable of expressing love and tenderness.

Even her feelings for Boyd were different. He stirred her in ways that Gary never had. Just the sight of him tickled her senses. Every time she looked at him, she wanted his arms around her. She would find herself reliving his inflaming kisses while stamping books in the library, feeling again the firmness of his lips against hers, the velvety softness of his tongue in her mouth.

Not only was the excitement of being with Boyd keener, but the deep happiness he brought her seemed truer. They were good companions, a couple who enjoyed the same things. They talked enthusiastically about many subjects and listened attentively to each other. Even their pauses were comfortable. They shared a feeling of silent togetherness.

They had something really special, Mia suddenly realized. Something one didn't throw away for the sake of a silly scruple. Sure, she might get hurt again—no risk, no gain. But the happiness she and Boyd could give each other was worth the risk.

Mia hurried. If she was going to start feeling sad about Boyd, she'd better look for the toboggan and exercise her melancholy away. She wondered briefly if she could handle the long sled by herself. It seemed to Mia that she had always used it with someone else, even sometimes her father. It was worth a look, anyway, she decided. If necessary, she could give some of the kids on the hill a ride.

She intended to go directly to the shed, but as she approached the cabin, she noticed a thick plume of smoke coming out of the chimney. Her first thought was *fire*.

Mia ran the rest of the way, her gaze fixed on the cabin. There was no sign of flames, yet the smoke was much thicker than her banked fire should have produced.

She quickly inserted her key in the door and opened it. Then she stood stock-still, listening. A sound of metal against metal came from the miniscule kitchen off the living room. Mia walked silently to the fire-place and grabbed the poker. Just as quietly she crossed the room and stood on the threshold of the kitchen.

To her amazement, Boyd was there, bending over the stove, the crosses and diamonds on his brown and white ski sweater stretched wide by his broad shoulders. He was spooning beans into a saucepan. He looked up when he heard her and glanced at the poker. "Hey, it's only me. You can put that thing down." He pointed to the can of beans. "You didn't leave any porridge when you went for your walk."

"And you're not Goldilocks. Do you know I could have you arrested for breaking and entering?"

"Enter, I did," Boyd said airily. "Break, I didn't."

"How did you get in? There's only one entrance, and all the windows were closed."

"I used a plastic credit card in the door lock."

Waggling his dark eyebrows humorously, he intoned in the fruity voice of a TV announcer, "Credit opens doors to all the things you wanted but thought you couldn't afford. Shouldn't you apply for your credit card today?"

Mia turned her head away to hide a radiant smile. Her heart was thumping like a wild thing against her ribs. She felt herself overflowing with happiness. Boyd couldn't help but notice. If it were night and the lights were turned off, Mia was sure she'd glow in the dark.

Boyd lit the burner under the pan. "Want some?"

Mia nodded. "I'm hungry. It's the mountain air."

"I'll cook the franks, too, then. We'll have to go to the store later on," he added matter-of-factly. "I guess you weren't expecting me."

"I certainly wasn't." Oh, but yes she was, her wicked heart answered. "How did you get here?" she asked. "The Lamborghini's not outside."

"I left it in the garage in town and took a taxi. Your mom told me about the road I'd have to take to get to the cabin, so I decided not to risk it."

"When did she tell you this?"

"Early this morning. I couldn't stand having you mad at me. So I broke a social rule and called your house very early."

Mia was thrilled that Boyd had cared enough to come, but felt just enough doubt about a relationship with him to keep from throwing herself into his arms.

"I'm not mad at you, Boyd. I just needed time to be by myself. There were things I wanted to think about. If you like, I'll drive you back to town after lunch. You can pick up your car and return to the city."

"I'm afraid I can't. The fanbelt on the Lamborghini broke. They're going to have to send all the way to Milan for another one." Boyd looked around the cabin. "I may be here for months."

"Sixty minutes is more like it. There's a little hotel in town. *If* your car is really inoperable."

"I get very unhappy in hotels."

"*I* get very unhappy having uninvited guests."

"Even if they're gourmet cooks?" Boyd peered down at the stove. "The franks and beans are ready."

"I'll put them on plates. There's no table in this small kitchen, so we'll eat in the living room."

"It's like old times," Boyd said facetiously as they sat down and put their plates on the redwood coffee table. "Sitting on a couch together in front of a fire."

Mia jabbed at her hot dog. "I'm not sentimental." Remembering their passionate kisses in Boyd's condo, she wished there were another place in the room to sit and eat. With Boyd couches led to trouble. And now she had to be doubly on guard—against herself as well as him.

He moved closer to her. She could feel his body heat and the nearness of his muscular thighs, could smell the delicious manly scent of him. Sizzling flames of desire swept through her. She couldn't resist him. She was the moth drawn to the flame.

But resisting him was a matter of principle. She couldn't allow herself to fall into Boyd Baxter's arms every time they sat next to each other on a couch.

Her ski sweater would be her armor, Mia decided. When Boyd peeled his off with the comment "Aren't you hot?" she said. "No," although she could feel her forehead beading with perspiration.

Boyd gave her a wicked, knowing sidelong glance. He let his gaze rove over her form, outlined softly but unmistakably under the heavy sweater. Then he made a production out of taking a clean handkerchief from his pocket and wiping her brow with it.

"You're apt to get heat stroke sitting in front of the fire with all that wool on you."

"I really don't mind," Mia said airily. "Coffee?"

"No thanks." If he had only sixty minutes, he wasn't going to waste any of them drinking coffee. "I'll clear the plates away." He saw Mia glance at the other chairs in the room. "On second thought, maybe we'll just leave them here." He didn't want her escaping from the couch while he was in the kitchen.

He turned to her and said earnestly, "I'd like to talk some more about the deal I made with my dad. I want everything between us to be open and honest."

"That's exactly the way I feel, Boyd, but I don't think you've—"

"Wait. Let me explain further. I couldn't see any way to get Dad to give up the motorcycle except through his love for Julia. That's when I made the deal to write all his material for him if he'd sell the motorcycle. Dad's a great guy. He really loves your mom and would do anything for her, but he has his male vanity. He insisted as part of the deal that I not tell Julia I was writing his jokes. He also asked me not to tell you, because he was afraid you would tell your mom. I didn't think you would, so I didn't promise him. But as I told you before, every time I tried to tell you, something intervened."

"I understand, Boyd," Mia said warmly. "I'm grateful to you for getting rid of the motorcycle." Her slim shoulders moved in a little shudder of dismay. "I worried all the time about them too. If I had known your dad wasn't even a good driver . . ." Mia left the rest of the thought unsaid. What could have happened to the elderly couple in the fast-moving freeway traffic was just too horrible to contemplate.

"By the way, Julia knows," Mia continued. "I started to tell her last night, but she's known all along that you've been writing the new material."

"Really?" Boyd said. "How did she find out?"

"She didn't believe all Romney's excuses for selling the motorcycle. At the same time she noticed the improvement in her material. You were the logical answer to the puzzle."

"Did she say anything about this to Romney?"

Mia shook her head. "She wanted to save his pride, so she went along with the lie."

"There are good lies and bad lies, Mia. Lying to protect the happiness of someone you love, which is what Julia is doing for Romney, isn't evil."

"It isn't evil, but it also isn't honest," Mia retorted.

Boyd shrugged. The ripple effect on his long-sleeved turtleneck fascinated Mia. With effort she tore her gaze from his powerful chest and leaned forward to remove the luncheon plates.

Boyd grabbed her wrist and pulled her back on the couch. "The dishes can wait, Mia. I have something important to tell you."

Mia turned toward him. His hand was still on her wrist, encircling the narrow bones in a warm, protective ring. She was so intent on what he was going to say, she didn't think to shake it off.

"I'm ready to make you a promise," Boyd said

quietly. "I won't write any more of Julia's material. From now on she and Romney are on their own."

Mia was stunned. "How about your deal with your dad?"

"I'll explain the situation to him. He'll understand." Boyd stared into the fire. "But maybe I won't let Julia know that I'm no longer writing her material. That way, if Romney's stuff bombs, she'll blame me, not him."

"Boyd!" Mia exclaimed sharply. "Julia doesn't need to be protected from the truth anymore than I do."

A boyish grin flashed swiftly across Boyd's handsome face. "You're right, Mia."

By this time Mia felt as if she was literally dying of the heat. She didn't know how much longer she could keep the heavy ski sweater on.

She suddenly remembered the sled she had set out to find.

"I was planning to go sledding on a hill nearby, if I could find my old toboggan."

"That sounds like fun," Boyd said enthusiastically. "Where is the toboggan?"

"I hope it's in the storage shed behind the house."

"Let's go get it," Boyd said, getting up.

The cool air outside refreshed Mia immediately. A blue jay chattered in a pine tree overhead. The sky was a clear, cloudless blue, and the sun was just warm enough to feel good on her face. As always she felt a special contentment at being with Boyd, swinging along in a fast walk beside him, the two of them unconsciously matching their rhythms to each other.

Mia unlocked the heavy padlock on the shed door. She switched on a light in the small, windowless building. Standing beside Boyd, she looked around.

Memories! Memories! she thought, as her gaze traveled over an old, unstrung tennis racket, a striped canvas hammock hanging from a nail, the guitar she had once taken lessons on, and a stack of children's books. Then she saw the long, flat-bottomed sled standing against a wall.

"There it is," she said happily.

Boyd lifted the sled and ran his finger along the thin boards that curved upward at one end. "It's a beauty. Whoever built it used fine wood."

"My dad," Mia said. "He didn't put on the handrails that real toboggans have because the hills here are so low. He just made it to hold a lot of children."

"Your mom told me you used to come up here often and have parties when your dad was alive."

Mia nodded pensively. "Those were happy years. I was lucky, I had a happy childhood." Her voice lifted in a merry lilt. "Hey, we'd better hurry while there's still some snow on that hill."

Boyd carried the sled to the hill. "There's no rudder on the toboggan, so let's be glad there are no trees," Boyd said.

They climbed to the top, dodging the children who were coasting down. Boyd led them to a spot on the slope where there wasn't a sled in sight.

"Ready?" Boyd shouted.

"Let her roll!" Mia answered on the rising note of a laugh.

They leapt aboard, Boyd pushing off, and started a long delirious descent, gathering speed as they went. Mia felt as though they were taking wing, flying through the air. She tightened her grip on Boyd's waist and slanted her body in the same direction he did, to steer the toboggan.

When they reached the bottom of the hill, Mia cried out, "Glorious! Let's do it again."

They mounted the hill several more times and slid down, experiencing the same exhilaration. But the hill soon became too crowded. They lost their isolated spot, and Boyd was afraid of running into a child.

"Let's go back to the cabin," he said. The sunshine had disappeared behind a sudden heap of gray clouds, and the air instantly became cooler. Mia felt a longing for the coziness of the warm fire. The bottoms of her flannel-lined blue jeans were wet and had begun to chafe her ankles.

"Good idea. I'm beginning to feel cold. Aren't you?"

He laughed. "I guess we're just a couple of true Californians. When the temperature drops below seventy, forget it!"

Boyd leaned the sled against the wall of the cabin. "I'll put it away later," he said. "First let's get warm." He took the keys from her hand and opened the front door. In two long, easy strides, he had reached the stone fireplace. Grabbing the poker, he rearranged the still-glowing logs, then placed another oak log in a strategic position. The flames shot up immediately, and the cabin was filled with the fragrant aroma of burning wood.

Mia noticed the luncheon dishes on the redwood coffee table. She reached for them. "I'll wash these while you're fooling around with the fire. The cabin doesn't have a dishwasher."

But Boyd grabbed the plates from her hand. "The fire doesn't need any tending now, but you're turning a lovely pale shade of blue with the cold. Why don't you strip and take a hot shower, while I do the dishes."

Mia hesitated. On the one hand, she realized that Boyd made her feel cared for and cherished—something Gary, ever attentive to his own comfort, never had—but on the other, the idea of taking a shower in such close quarters with Boyd suggested an intimacy she hadn't perpared herself for.

Boyd reached out a hand and took the bottom of her heavy ski sweater between his thumb and index finger. "That's pretty wet, Mia. You'd better get warmed up so you don't catch cold."

Another chill rippled through Mia in spite of the warm fire.

Noticing it, Boyd said, "You're damp as a snowflake." Before she could stop him, he had inserted his hands under the sweater and pulled it off over her head. The feel of his hands along her sides and over her breasts made her senses flame with a deliriously exciting need for him.

Mutely she took the sweater from Boyd and left the room. She took dry clothes out of a small bureau in the downstairs bedroom and entered the bathroom next to it.

She stood under the shower and let the needles of warm water strike her skin. As her body relaxed, her mind filled with all the wonderful events of the day. She still couldn't quite get over the fact that Boyd had come to her. She knew that his promise to stop writing Julia's material had been a sacrifice on his part. But most of all she remembered the feel of his body as she pressed against him on the toboggan. Even through the bulk of their winter clothes she could feel the hard muscles that were a testament to his virility. They formed an exciting contrast to the sensitive, slender-fingered hands that had caressed her so thrillingly as they removed her ski sweater.

Mia stepped out of the shower and gently toweled herself. She blow-dried her hair until it hugged her head in a shapely ebony wave. Then she slipped on a wool jersey caftan in a luscious shade of tomato-red. She applied red lipstick, outlining, then filling in the full curves of her smooth, upward-turning lips.

Boyd was poking the fire when she entered the room. He looked up and a glow of ardent appreciation shone in his eyes. "You look very beautiful," he murmured.

Mia advanced toward him, holding her hands out to the roaring fire. "That was a good idea of yours to warm up under a shower."

Boyd took her hands. "Still cold?"

Mia laughed a little, trying to ignore the trembling that had started inside her at his touch, hoping he wouldn't notice the flush on her cheeks, the pulse she felt beating wildly at the base of her throat.

Almost unconsciously, it seemed, he began to stroke her wrist, his forefinger and thumb keeping up a steady hypnotic rhythm. As light and reassuring a caress as it was, Mia felt as though her whole body was leaning into it, focusing on the delightful sensation.

His bright sapphire eyes looked deep into hers. "Have you forgiven me, Mia? I didn't mean to deceive you. I did it out of love for you."

Mia's heart fluttered like a wild bird at his declaration of love. She wasn't even sure that she had heard him correctly. "Oh, Boyd," she murmured, "I was never really *that* angry with you. I knew you had done the right thing in getting rid of the motorcycle."

Boyd looked at her with mock severity. "You're missing the main point." He scooped her into his arms and buried his face in the scented hollow of her neck. "Which is that I love you, adore you, want you."

Mia inhaled sharply. How did she ever think she could do without this man? The feel of his strong features against her soft skin, the familiar clean, spicy smell of him, were like a glorious homecoming.

He cradled her head between his palms then, and his mouth mated with hers in a consciousness-stealing kiss. His lips were warm and compelling on hers, but there was no arrogance or demand in the kiss. It was a tender, sensual caress that drew from Mia an overwhelming desire to respond.

She parted her lips and let the tip of her tongue touch the sharp white ridge of his teeth. A low groan broke from Boyd as his arms closed tighter around her. She was so sweet to taste, so warm and responsive, he felt consumed by the raging fire she sparked. His tongue met hers and followed it back into her mouth, engaging it in a slow, stroking duel.

Then he lifted his mouth from hers and spread a line of kisses over her cheek and chin, and down her long delicate neck. Mia's breath began coming in small shallow gasps. Her excitement gave rise to a compelling need to touch him.

She explored his earlobes with caressing touches of her fingers. Then she smoothed out his thick, dark brows, which secretly thrilled her as a sign of masterfulness and virility. His eyes remained closed as she traced the ruler-straight length of his nose to his upper lip. As her fingertips skated across his lips, he kissed each one in turn.

"Wait, I'm not finished," Mia said with a little laugh. She inserted her finger in the cleft in his chin. "That's what I like about you. I think it's cute. Kissable!" She bent forward and pressed her lips to the narrow fissure.

"Let's play fair here," Boyd growled. "Where's that dimple of yours?"

It took tremendous effort but, with eyes sparkling as she teased him, Mia managed to suppress her dimple behind a perfectly straight, sober face.

"Okay, I guess I'll have to go looking for something else to kiss."

As Mia waited in breathless anticipation, his fingers slipped from her arm and over her hip. He flattened his hand on the curve of her stomach then, and Mia held her breath. When he moved it upward and let it skim over her breasts, she relaxed, giving herself over to the pulsing excitement that bubbled up inside her.

With slow, sensual movements, he unzipped her caftan and moved his hand inside to cup her breast. Releasing her bra, Boyd groaned and cradled her closer. He took one nipple between his thumb and forefinger and chafed it gently. Then he bent his head to kiss the throbbing peak.

Mia shivered in his arms. She felt almost delirious with feelings she had never known before. Her legs shifted restlessly as she lowered her head to press her lips against the warm column of his throat.

As he moved to the other breast and drew its dusky rose nipple into his mouth, he slipped one hand below her waist to caress her back. When Mia curled more tightly against him, he slid his tongue lightly into her mouth.

"Is there a bed in this place or do we have to use a tree house?"

"There's a bed, but it's not made up. There are sleeping bags in the loft."

"One's all we need," Boyd murmured, curving his hand around her soft derriere.

Tenderly he led her across the room and followed her up the ladder into the sleeping loft. Mia took a royal blue sleeping bag with a red and black checkered, cotton flannel lining out of the cupboard. Boyd unzipped it and laid it on the carpeted floor.

The flames from the fire below cast huge dancing shadows around them as Boyd quickly, gently, finished undressing her.

"Hop into the sleeping bag, sweet. It's chilly up here."

Mia watched Boyd shed his own clothes with a speed and roughness very different from the cherishing way he had undressed her. As he stood completely naked in front of her, the firelight flickered over his magnificent body, imbuing it with a color and radiance she found breathtaking.

"You look like a caveman," Mia said with a little laugh.

He looked down into her luminous eyes, then slid into the sleeping bag beside her. "And you are the most beautiful cavewoman I have ever seen."

As his warmth covered her and his arousal pressed against her belly, Mia gasped.

He drew slightly away. "What is it, darling?"

"Nothing. You're just so . . . *male*."

Boyd's chest shook with laughter. "You ain't seen nothing yet, baby."

His hand flicked lazily over her nipples again. He moved it lower to caress the flatness of her belly, then lower still.

A soft sigh escaped Mia's lips as his fingers stroked along her leg, then slowly traced the sensitive sides of her inner thigh. She writhed against him as he found the throbbing center of her arousal, and she pleaded with him in dark whispers to take her.

"Not yet, darling. Not quite yet," Boyd murmured huskily.

He continued to caress her leisurely, his hands arousing her until she became a wild thing, kissing him passionately, tugging at the springy hair on his chest, running eager hands down his slim flanks.

Boyd groaned, then pulled her on top of him. Mia nearly sobbed with satisfaction as he thrust deep within her, her knees bending to accommodate him. He lifted his head so that his tongue could play with her breasts, and Mia pressed them closer to him. Every movement of his body brought her to new, higher levels of hot, glowing joy until Mia wondered if she could bear it.

His hands at her waist held her firmly in place, intensifying his pleasure and hers. Finally, together, they spun higher and higher, reaching an unknown realm of frenzied rapture.

When at last their passion was spent, Mia sighed.

"What is it, darling?"

Mia glanced at Boyd's bare chest and down at her own love-swollen breasts.

She uttered a low, easy, musical laugh that always made Boyd desire her. "I love you, Boyd, with every single bit of my being. I think I must be the happiest cavewoman in the whole wide world."

Boyd pulled her into his arms again. "That makes *me* one happy caveman, because I love you totally and completely."

They lay entwined together throughout the night. Mia awoke when Boyd planted a kiss on her soft skin. She pressed up against him, her whole body delighting in the feel of his hard, muscular form. Boyd took her without further preliminaries, and Mia was surprised to find her own desire so easily renewed.

Exhausted and sated from lovemaking, they slept nestled against each other, until the pale golden sunlight of a mountain morning flooded the cabin.

Seven

Mia and Boyd delayed returning to the city until the last possible moment. Then Mia drove Boyd to the little town where he had garaged his Lamborghini.

"That fanbelt arrived from Milan awfully fast," she said archly.

Boyd's face became a study in innocence. "Perhaps they found one locally."

Driving home, Mia kept the car radio on. The love songs didn't sound insipid to her for once. She hummed along with the music, hugging the "I love you's" she and Boyd had exchanged close to her heart like a delicious secret. She felt lucky and happy in love.

Instead of rain, she drove through a golden sunset that gilded the low hills on one side and burnished the smooth, calm Pacific on the other.

Julia was gone when Mia got home, the usual note propped up on the kitchen table. The phone rang even before she had finished reading the note. It was Boyd.

"Mia, I just got home," Boyd began, his voice low, somber. "There was a message on my machine. An urgent one. A deal I've had cooking for some time in San Francisco is about to close. I have to fly up there right away. Any chance of your going with me, Mia?"

"I'd love to, but I can't take time off from the library without advance notice. How long will you be gone?"

"Anywhere from five days to a week. This is a package deal involving several properties, and it will take some careful negotiating. I'll call you every night from San Francisco."

They talked for several minutes more, exchanging words of love and laughing. But after hanging up, Mia felt a terrible bleakness of spirit descend on her. She felt as bereft as if there had been a death in the family. She would miss Boyd's laughter and companionship. Her body would ache with longing for him—and he wouldn't be there. He'd be gone.

Before her depression could get a deeper hold on her, Mia forced herself to chase it away. Boyd said he loved her, and Boyd wasn't the kind of man to make serious declarations lightly. She was being silly. In the very unlikely event that he ever did want to break off their relationship, he would come right out and tell her. He wouldn't do it be sneaking away . . .

Story time had just ended, and children scrambled out to look for books to check out. One young mother stayed behind to ask Mia to recommend a book for her little girl.

While Mia talked, she thought about how wonderful it would be to have Boyd's child, to watch the unfolding of the child's intelligence and personality every day.

A movement at the rear of the large room, where a cardboard cutout of Tom Sawyer stood, caught her attention. Boyd was unfolding his long frame from a chair which was much too small for him and coming her way. Boyd obviously had been the late arrival, she realized.

Mia grinned, her whole body flushing and tingling. Waves of excitement washed over her.

The mother talking to her looked at Mia curiously. She broke off the conversation with repeated "thank you's" and edged her way toward the open door.

"Boyd! Why didn't you let me know you were coming?"

He clasped her small hands in his. "I wanted to surprise you. I was checking to see how you'd read to *our* kids."

Boyd's thinking so closely paralleled the ideas she had just had that Mia was startled. He dropped her hands and pulled her toward him. "I missed you so, Mia," he said softly, then kissed her with a fervent sweetness that told eloquently just how much he'd missed her.

Their parents had begged them to come to the Laff-A-Minute, and Mia and Boyd felt they couldn't refuse any longer. They arrived early and found the club transformed with green crepe paper festooning the walls and clusters of green balloons, like swollen grapes, hanging from the ceiling.

Mia was baffled. "It's not St. Patrick's Day, is it, Boyd?"

A waiter going by with a small black derby on his head, a green bow tie, and a white apron tied around his waist said, "Tonight is Irish night. We've got a guest comedian who's come all the way from Dublin."

"Won't you have your regulars?" Mia asked, disappointed. Julia hadn't mentioned there would be an Irish night at the club.

"Oh sure, they'll warm up the audience for Pat O'Malley." He put his large metal tray down on the table. "What'll you guys have to drink? We've got lots of specials with crème de menthe tonight. Concoctions such as 'Killarney Memories,' 'Irish Smiles,' 'The Druid's Lament.'"

Boyd's face showed his distaste. "They're all green, I gather."

"Green as the hills of old Ireland," the boy answered, tossing back a lock of blond hair.

"I'll have a glass of white wine and hold the creme de menthe. Mia?"

"The same, please."

Mia looked around the room. "There are lots of people here for a change," she said in a pleased voice. She was about to add another comment when the emcee's voice pierced the air. "*And heeere's Laff-A-Minute's favorite stand-up comic, Julia Taylor. Give the little lady a big hand, folks.*"

The applause was spontaneous and sustained. There were even shouts of "Hey, Julia!"

Mia gazed at Boyd, wide-eyed. "She's getting a lot of applause."

"She's been put in an important spot, too, right before the Irish comedian."

"You and your funny jokes," Mia said.

"It's all over with now. I've already let Romney know that I wouldn't be writing any more of his material."

Boyd had hated pulling out on his dad, leaving him in the lurch. Now he dreaded witnessing the results of his action. There wasn't another person he would have done it for except Mia. She was the most uncompromising person when it came to honesty he had ever known. He didn't go along with all her ideas, but he admired and loved her for her sense of honor. He had no chance to say more to Mia now, though, because Julia was speaking.

Julia was using a creditable Irish brogue to tell a few Irish jokes, all of which got hearty laughs. Then, deferring to the guest comic, the true Irish comedian, she dropped both the brogue and the Irish stories.

Boyd was tense watching her. This, he told himself, was the acid test. The audience might have thought her Irish act appealing, but now Julia was telling Romney's jokes.

The beginning of the routine was weak, or maybe it just seemed so, he thought, because of the richness of the Irish material. Still, in spite of the paucity of laughs, Julia looked relaxed and confident.

Boyd saw his father at his usual ringside table. Romney looked as serene and content as a well-fed baby.

What do they know that I don't know? Boyd wondered.

Fifteen minutes later amid deafening applause, he

had his answer. Romney and Julia knew that their jokes were good. Better than good—clever, witty, and yet human too.

Boyd hailed a passing derby-hatted waiter and pointed to their empty glasses.

"So what do you think?" he asked Mia.

"Incredible. I wouldn't believe it if I hadn't seen it. The material was sharp. Julia delivered it with perfect timing. They were a complete success." Mia glanced suspiciously at Boyd. "Are you sure you didn't slip a couple of your jokes in?"

Boyd raised his hands in mock defense. "Only the one about why the chicken crossed the road."

The waiter set down their glasses of wine. "Top of the evening to you, sir."

Boyd burrowed in his pocket for his wallet. "You don't know it, but it's more like the bottom of the ninth."

"We're having a Baseball day when the Series starts," the kid said brightly.

"I'm not sure we'll be back," Boyd mumbled.

The Irish comedian came on next, his thick brogue rolling through the room, his timing professionally perfect as he waited for the last wavelet of laughter to pass before starting a new joke. When he had finished, the audience spontaneously got to its feet for a standing ovation. He told a few more jokes, then he hopped off the stage and left the room.

"Wasn't he tremendous?" Mia asked, her eyes sparkling with enthusiasm.

Boyd nodded wearily. "I suppose so, only sometimes I think I'm losing my appetite for comedy. Here come the folks."

•

Julia and Romney, aglow from their success, approached the table. Boyd pulled out two chairs.

"Wasn't Pat O'Malley simply grand?" Julia asked.

"He was," Mia answered. "Speaking of jokes, the ones you wrote for Mom were very good, Romney."

"I'm half Irish. No true Irishman can resist a joke. In my case it took a while for me to learn to write them, but I think I've finally got the knack."

Everyone agreed: Julia with her hazel eyes flashing with pride; Boyd with a combination of filial pride and wry amusement at the way things had turned out; and Mia out of a sense of fair play. She couldn't deny that Romney's jokes were funny. She only wished he had found some other aspiring lady comic to bestow them on.

Romney swept the three of them with his slightly faded but still piercing gaze. "I guess you all know that it was Boyd who really helped me hone my style. Without those jokes of his for me to learn from, I wouldn't have made it. And my apologies to you ladies for any minor deception involved." If he had had a hat to doff, he would have tipped it to Julia and Mia.

"Well, your ladies weren't deceived for long, Romney," Julia said. "I caught on fairly quickly, and Mia did too."

Romney looked hurt. "What made you catch on so fast? Were my original jokes really so lousy?"

"No, dear, the fact that you sold your motorcycle for no very convincing reason that I could see."

How careful her mother was of Romney's feelings, Mia thought. And her mother's sensitivity was reciprocated by Romney. They never seemed to quarrel, to misunderstand each other, to feel unappreciated.

Suddenly as if from out of nowhere, a curious sound issued from Romney. *"Brrm . . . brrm . . . vroom . . . Vroom . . . Brrmm!"*

People even at faraway tables turned to look at the man who had apparently lost all his marbles.

But Julia understood. She smiled nostalgically. "It was fun, Romney. I adored wearing a black leather jacket and that Darth Vader helmet with the visor. And I did feel perfectly safe with you no matter how fast you went. But we might never have known what a gifted comedy writer you were if you hadn't given up the motorcycle. And that's more important than a 'Brrm . . . brrm . . . vroom,' isn't it?"

Romney sighed. "You're right, Julia. And when we get too lonesome for life on the road, we can always rent motorcycle movies from the video library."

He rose from the table. "Well, Julia and I are off to the Zebra Lounge for an hour or so. It's been a big evening, and we have to unwind. We'll stop back here on our way home. I promised Mr. Baker a ride. His car's in the shop."

"How about inviting Mia and me to the disco, Dad?"

"Oh, I don't think you kids would like it," Julia said quickly. "It's terribly noisy. The music's not that good. The dance floor's always packed. . . ."

"We've been to discos," Boyd said dryly. "I can't believe the Zebra Lounge is that different."

"I was wrong," Boyd muttered to Mia as they walked into what looked like a giant cage being shaken and pounded from the outside by some infernal machine. "The Zebra Lounge *is* different."

When she got her bearings, Mia saw that everything was striped in black and white—the walls, the ceiling, the floor, the furniture, even the bar. Deafening music added to the disorienting effect, while a crowd of gyrating dancers bounced around like drops of water on a hot stove.

"Isn't this *fun?*" Julia yelled above the din, looking up into Mia's and Boyd's faces to see how they were responding.

"I don't know, Julia, I think we might be too old for this scene," Boyd said.

"Nonsense! Everyone here is your age, give or take a few years. Romney and I are the standouts."

"There are discos for seniors," Mia began cautiously.

"Slow!" Julia said contemptuously. She looked at the dance floor with longing. "I can hardly wait to get out there and boogie. Romney, what do you say?"

Romney's eyes lit up with pleasure. "Sure thing. Why don't you kids grab a table. We'll find you later."

"So here we are again, sitting at a table while our parents are *participating*," Boyd said as they sat down and ordered drinks.

Mia sighed. "You know that saying, youth is wasted on the young."

"It certainly is on us—tonight," Boyd said with a big grin.

Mia knew what he meant. She returned his grin with a secret, complicitous smile.

"Shall we join our *elderly* parents?" he asked,

indicating the dance floor. "There they are," Boyd mouthed in the direction of Mia's ear.

Mia followed his glance. Romney and Julia had claimed a little corner for themselves. Was it the same corner week after week? Mia wondered. Other dancers smiled at them and sometimes stopped to watch the elderly couple as they danced at a slow tempo all their own. People at a nearby table applauded at the end of the set.

"How come your dad isn't short of breath now?" Mia asked.

"They're not really moving much," Boyd answered. "I asked him about that, and he reassured me he always felt just fine." Boyd looked around and rolled his eyes. "Not that the Zebra Lounge is the place I'd recommend for senior citizens."

"They're heading for the table now. Perhaps they rest more than we think."

"I certainly hope so."

The music began again. Boyd pulled Mia to him, and they started to dance. Mia didn't know if the music was fast or slow, loud or soft. All she knew was that she was in Boyd's arms again, synchronizing her movements with his, twisting and turning in rhythmic patterns reminiscent of the act of love.

"You turn me on," Boyd whispered in her ear. "I want you. I can't go on without you. Let's go someplace and let me make a dishonest woman of you."

Her eyes sparkling with humor, Mia put her hand to her heart. "*Dishonest?*"

Boyd grinned down at her. "Wrong word. Let's go back to square one. My condo lacks a sleeping loft, but I have sleeping bags and a fireplace, and I could probably hunt up a can of beans somewhere."

As Mia searched for an answer, the amplifiers were turned up, and the only language being spoken on the dance floor was body language.

After a short while Boyd said impatiently, "Let's get our parents out of here. This is no place for them. I can't even *see* them for the cigarette smoke, for Pete's sake. Are they dancing again?"

"No, they're sitting at the table, holding hands. They look pooped."

"Good, then it's home and beddy-bye for all of us."

Which homes? Mia wondered. Did Julia go to Romney's condo? Should she go to Boyd's?

As Boyd and Mia approached the table, Boyd said teasingly, "We're tired, Mom and Dad. Can't we go home now?"

A little thrill went through Mia when Boyd said "Mom" and she caught the gleam in Julia's eye.

Romney turned to Julia and laughed. "Well, I guess the kids are too young for nightclubs."

"*These* kids are," Boyd said. "Besides, there's enough tar in my lungs already to resurface Wilshire Boulevard. Shall we go? We can leave together and pick up our cars in the parking lot."

Mia looked at Boyd and Romney. "I suppose I could go home with Mom and save you both detours." Even her own mother gave her a dirty look at that suggestion. "Oh, well, detours it is," Mia added brightly.

"I've got a great detour planned for us," Boyd said as he settled her in the Lamborghini.

Boyd's masterful way of taking over thrilled Mia,

but she felt in a playful mood. "I don't like to get too far off the beaten path, Boyd."

"This place is right on the beaten path. In fact, we'll be lucky if we can get a place to park."

Fifteen minutes later a small car with a vanity license plate that spelled out *I'm Tuf* ceded a space to the Lamborghini. "Aha!" Boyd exclaimed humorously. "Intimidation, that's the key."

As they left the car, the wistful strains of a calliope filled the night air with a hauntingly lovely Strauss waltz.

"It's the merry-go-round!" Mia exclaimed with delight.

A big green frog with a polka dot bow, a tiger with a purple and gold saddle, a swan boat, and one wild-looking black charger with a tossed mane and red lips drawn back over long white teeth flew by under flashing lights and mirrors, past wood panels painted with Gibson girls in bathing dresses and a mermaid with hair the color of goldfish.

"How did you know that I love the merry-go-round?" Mia asked.

"I know everything about you," he murmured, brushing his lips against her cool, soft cheek.

"You don't know which animal I prefer."

"Yes, I do." He pulled her roughly into his arms and kissed her briefly, explosively. "Me!"

"Wrong again." Mia said, laughing. "It's that gorgeous tiger."

"He's yours," Boyd said. "I'm jumping on that black charger. It's a shame there are so few of these beautiful old carousels left. This one was built in 1900 in New York. It was used in a little resort in Massachusetts until just a few years ago when it was renovated and brought here."

They bought two tickets at the booth, and Mia started to climb on the back of a ferocious looking tiger with sharp claws. With one hand around her waist and the other on her rump, Boyd lifted her up.

Mia fixed him with a stern eye. "That really wasn't necessary. I've been riding merry-go-rounds all my life." She smiled. "That doesn't mean I've been on a merry-go-round all my life."

Boyd looked down at her humorously. "Well, I have, since I met you. Lady on a tiger," he mused aloud. He buckled the leather strap around Mia's waist. "I can't let anything happen to you," he said with a smile.

The sound system cranked out the opening bars of the "Tennessee Waltz," the bell rang again, and the merry-go-round started to revolve.

Boyd leaped onto his handsome black stallion with rolling eyes and fiery red nostrils, saying, "I'll race you."

"Very funny. I have a better idea. Let's see who gets the first brass ring."

"You're on!" Boyd dug his heels into the horse's flanks and struck his neck with the flat of his hand.

Mia whispered encouraging words into her tiger's ear and for one silly moment imagined he was surging ahead.

When they drew abreast of the stick holding the rings, Mia stood high in the tiger's stirrups and reached with all her might for the brass ring dangling there—but she missed.

A second later she turned and looked at Boyd. He

was holding up a ring between his finger and thumb and flashing her a victory grin.

"Oh!" Mia sputtered. "It's unfair. Your horse is higher, and you're taller."

"All's fair in love . . ." When the ride came to an end, Boyd reached up his arms and lifted Mia down. "Do you like saltwater taffy?"

"Love it."

"Then let's head toward the bay. There's a shop there that sells it."

They walked through the theme park, past shops built of factory-weathered gray shingles. Tourists lined up to buy souvenir T-shirts, homemade fudge, expensive wooden toys, and decorative shells.

There was street entertainment: Jugglers, fire-eaters, unicycle riders, mimes. Their hats, placed in front of them, were rapidly filling with money. Although Mia and Boyd didn't stop to watch any of them, Boyd made generous contributions as they walked along.

The saltwater taffy shop was off the beaten track in a dark corner of the park facing the bay.

Boyd bought a package of delicately swirled pink and white candy, and they went to a nearby bench outside to eat it.

"It's so peaceful here!" Mia exclaimed.

The ficus trees around them absorbed the sounds of the shoppers and entertainers. Only the sweet waltz music of the merry-go-round reached them. Occasionally a sight-seeing boat, festive and golden with lights, would glide across the bay. Otherwise the water was dark under a starry sky.

"Can you waltz?" Boyd asked.

Mia made a face in the dark. "Dancing school.

Mom made me go when I was twelve. I belonged to something called a cotillion, if you can believe it. The girls wore white cotton gloves and black patent leather shoes."

He laughed. "The same for me. We had bow ties on elastics that we used to snap at each other. We slicked our hair down with so much grease, we were instantly flammable."

Boyd stood and bowed from the waist. "May I have this dance?"

"Yes, I'd be delighted." Mia slipped into his arms like a ship into its mooring. The carousel was playing "The Blue Danube" waltz. Boyd held her close and guided her expertly around the small area of sidewalk between the bench and the water.

Mia was wearing a white silk dress splashed with big pink roses and delicate pale green leaves. It was deeply cut in a V-shape in back. Boyd's fingers splayed warmly and firmly across her smooth skin. Her soft breasts and firm belly and thighs gave under the push of his hard muscular frame as he held her close.

It was like floating on a cloud to move in such perfect union with Boyd. She ceased to have a separate identity, to be Mia Taylor. She was one with the man who had captured her heart and her body. It was an exciting yet reassuring feeling.

When the last plaintive strains of the music died on the soft night air, Boyd ended the dance in a low, old-fashioned dip and a kiss that added to the sweet, passionate desire growing within her.

Boyd kept his arms around Mia and settled her on the bench, nestled against him.

"With that taffy, I'm surprised you could open your mouth enough for a kiss," Mia said, laughing.

"I've been doing this for years," Boyd boasted. "Eating saltwater taffy and kissing girls. In case you don't believe me, I'll show you again."

Mia laughed and raised her hands in self-defense. "I believe you! I believe you!" She didn't think she could risk another kiss. She'd go up in a shower of lights and stars like the Fourth of July fireworks.

"I just want to see if your peppermint tastes like mine," Boyd muttered huskily.

He turned her in his arms and lifted her face with his palms for a kiss. It was long and slow and deep, compelling them to satisfy the passion that drew them to each other. Yet there was tenderness in the kiss, too, a tenderness that fueled their hunger so that they kissed again and again with desperate urgency.

Boyd tilted her chin up toward him. "Remember when I kissed the marshmallow off your lips at the beach?"

"Umm. I was squeaky clean."

"You're a little sticky with peppermint tonight," Boyd said.

"Do you choose your women on the basis of what they eat?"

"Sure, I have a sweet tooth." Suddenly, he nibbled at her lower lip. Mia began to laugh, and he kissed her again, joining their peppermint breaths.

When he lifted his mouth from hers, he took the fourth finger of her left hand and slipped the brass ring from the merry-go-round on it.

"What do you think, Mia?" he asked quietly.

"Yes, darling," Mia whispered. "I want to wear your brass ring forever."

"I don't think so," Boyd said humorously. "You can hardly keep it on your finger now. I'm going to replace it with a diamond ring."

A swell of happiness rushed through Mia. A lifetime with Boyd would be her future. They would always be together. His beloved face would be the last one she saw at night, the first in the morning.

As if reading her mind, Boyd said, "We'll have our own children's story hour at home."

Mia chuckled. "I know just the books to read to them."

Boyd smiled fondly, as if recalling a cherished memory. "You'll have to include *Alice in Wonderland.*"

"Of course! And you can teach them to play chess."

An expression of wonderment came into both their eyes.

"It looks as though we're closing a circle," Mia said tentatively.

Boyd knew immediately what she meant.

"Or continuing a tradition. Falling in love and founding a family. Doing 'Mom and Dad' things with the kids. But not all the time," Boyd added.

They came together slowly, as if recognizing that they were sharing a solemn moment. Boyd took her in his arms tenderly and sealed their pledges to each other with fervent kisses.

"Tell me again how much you love me. I want to hear it over and over again."

"I do love you, Boyd, more than I've ever loved any other human being."

He slid a finger beneath her chin and lifted her

face to his for another slow-motion kiss. When they finally broke away, Mia became aware of the silence around them. "I don't hear the merry-go-round," she commented.

"They're probably closing the park. We'd better go."

They got up and, with arms around each other, joined the stream of departing visitors.

"I'm dying to tell Mom the wonderful news," Mia said wistfully. "She'll be so happy."

"Romney will be too. He's very fond of you."

"Grandchildren! Romney and Julia will be deliriously happy!"

"Let's hurry home and give them the good news."

Eight

Mia was surprised and disappointed to find that her mother wasn't home when she got there. She debated over whether she should wait up so that she could share her happiness with her mother immediately, but decided against it.

She was in love with the most wonderful man in the world, and she was going to marry him, but she was also a working woman. Love or no love, she would have to open the library as usual early in the morning.

So, humming "The Blue Danube" waltz while taking a few dance steps, Mia got ready for bed.

Some latent uneasiness broke into a sweet dream of Boyd and woke Mia up during the night. She glanced at the clock. It was past two o'clock, and she hadn't heard the front door open or the whispered cooing of Romney and Julia in the hall.

To be certain, she got up and checked her mother's bed. It was empty.

Mia called Boyd. After the phone rang a long time, she heard a sleepy "Yes?"

Mia couldn't help but laugh at the little boy sound of his voice. She pictured him tousle-haired and yawning, and wished she were there with him. "You'd make a fine fireman, Boyd."

Boyd chuckled. "Is that what you called me up in the middle of the night to tell me? That I won't be accepted by the fire department?"

"Not exactly." She paused, hating to say the words because it would bring her fear out into the open, make it real. "Julia's not home. Do you know where your dad is?"

"No, I don't. But don't worry about them, Mia," Boyd said. "At least they're not killing themselves on a motorcycle."

"One of them could be lying on the floor of that disco with a slipped disk."

"There wouldn't be room to fall," Boyd said dryly. "Listen, why don't you go back to bed and stop worrying. Or better yet come back to *my* bed and let me smooth away all your little cares."

He could, too, Mia thought. One touch of his big hands and the world could go up in smoke for all she cared.

Just then Mia's call-waiting sounded.

"I've got another call," she said excitedly. "Maybe it's them. Hold on."

She pressed the receiver button of the phone and heard her mother's voice.

"Mia? I want you to get a lawyer right away." Julia's usual soft, precise voice came over the line sharp and quick.

"But we have a lawyer, Mom. Mr. Elliott. Should I

call him? And what do you need him for?" Mia's heart was beating fast. She feared the worst.

"Not Elliott. Romney and I need a criminal lawyer."

"A criminal lawyer! What have you done, Mother?"

"Nothing any other red-blooded, stand-up comic wouldn't have done. The police closed down the Laff-A-Minute right after we got back there tonight. They said they were serving drinks to minors. Well, that's just a bunch of hogwash. Romney and I practically live in the club, and never, never have we seen a minor served anything stronger than a Coke."

"But where are you?"

"Romney and I are in jail. The charge is disorderly conduct."

Mia had forgotten all about Boyd on the other line. The situation was so astounding, she could hardly take it all in. Two senior citizens arrested for disorderly conduct in a scruffy little comedy club?

In spite of the cold, hard stone of anxiety that seemed to have settled in the pit of her stomach, Mia forced herself to be calm. "What exactly did you and Romney do?"

"We objected to the accusation that the club had broken the law and particularly to them closing it down."

"How did you object, Mom?"

"Well, vociferously, of course. Mr. Baker has been very good to us. Moreover, the club was going to be my springboard to bigger and better places. But I couldn't move on if I didn't have a launching pad to move *from*, could I?"

"Neither you nor Romney became violent, did you?"

"Oh sure, they had to put a choke hold on Romney to subdue him. What's happened to your brains, Mia?"

"They're addled, Mom. I'm really terribly upset that you and Romney are in jail."

She didn't want to say so, but Mia was consumed with worry that her mother might suffer another heart attack under the stress of being arrested. But Julia's brisk, acerbic voice laid her anxiety to rest.

"I have to hang up now," Julia said. "There's a strange-looking man watching me. Tell Boyd about it and get down here as soon as possible, will you, please, dear? We're at the central police station."

When she depressed the receiver button of the phone, there was silence. A minute later the phone rang.

"You must have had a hot number on the other line," Boyd complained. "I held till my ear dropped off."

"Do you know a good criminal lawyer?"

"For you? What did you do? Reverse the Dewey decimal system?"

"Julia and Romney are in jail, and the Laff-A-Minute's been closed down."

"What for—bad jokes?"

"The cops allege the bartender at the club sold liquor to minors."

"Certainly not to Julia and Romney!"

"Boyd, I'm not joking. My mother and your dad are in jail at this very minute on a charge of disorderly conduct. As Julia put it, they objected vociferously when the police closed the club."

Boyd let out a long whistle. "I don't think they need a lawyer though. One look at them as disturbers of the peace and the judge will burst out laughing."

"Are you sure, Boyd? You're not just saying that to reassure me? I'm really terribly worried."

"Reasonably sure. I know some of the guys at the station. I think I can fix it up. All right if I pick you up in ten minutes?"

"Yes, I'll be ready."

She dressed quickly, ran a brush through her hair, put some lipstick on, and waited.

Boyd had gone to all the trouble of dressing in a three-piece business suit and shirt and tie. "I thought it might help if I looked ultrarespectable."

"I don't know, darling. I think you look strange, as though you just came out of a board meeting at three o'clock in the morning."

The Lamborghini sped through the empty streets. Boyd and Mia were silent for a while. Then Boyd said, "You know, I really wish you had kept a better eye on Julia. If there was something wrong going on at the club, she shouldn't have been there."

"Doesn't the same apply to Romney?"

"Well, Romney's a man. That's a little different."

"Really! Well, I think it's just as bad for a seventy-year-old man to be in the pokey as a woman, and if you had been doing your duty by your father he wouldn't be there."

"I don't want to quarrel with you, Mia, but I'd like to point out that Dad never got into trouble until he met your mom."

"Oh!" Mia gasped indignantly. "Now we're back to where we began—the woman as temptress."

"Let's just wait and see how this little incident turns out, shall we? The future always reveals itself."

"I think you've been reading too many fortune cookies," Mia said tartly.

"How about this?" Boyd said. "Elderly parents like rebellious teenagers—need wise counseling and careful attention."

"Very true. And who failed to give careful attention to his elderly parent?"

"Who didn't see that her mother was safely at home and in bed before two o'clock in the morning?"

They stalked into the police station without speaking to each other, their faces stiff with anger. Romney and Julia were in the squad room. Julia gave them a cheery wave, and Romney got up to shake hands.

The big room contained three desks, at which two male detectives and a policewoman were working. Other officers wandered in and out.

"Ron!" Boyd called out to an officer with long dark sideburns.

"Hey, Boyd, long time no see. What are you doing here?"

Boyd rolled his eyes heavenward. "I've come to bail some people out." He indicated Julia and Romney sitting side by side on a long, crowded wooden bench.

Mia sat down on another bench after a man in a smelly overcoat, held together with safety pins, went through an elaborate act of moving over.

Ron's sharp-featured angular face broke into a smile. "You're kidding! What did they do—cheat at bingo?"

"They objected a little too strongly to the Laff-A-Minute's being closed down for allegedly serving drinks to minors."

"Oh yeah? What were two old fogies—I mean, two senior citizens—doing at the Laff-A-Minute?"

"Mrs. Taylor is a stand-up comic there."

Ron did a double take, then jerked his head toward Mia, now sliding away from the man in the odiferous overcoat. "That her daughter?"

"Yes." Boyd introduced Ron to Mia as an old schoolfriend.

"What's your connection?" Ron asked Boyd.

"Mia's my fiancée."

"Listen, let me handle this," Ron said confidently. "You should all be on your way home in about five minutes."

Ron disappeared behind a door marked "Captain." Boyd sat down next to Mia but didn't take her hand. "Ron says he can get them out, so let's stop worrying."

Mia smiled with relief and attempted a joke. "I was afraid they wouldn't even be put in the same cell."

"Or they'd put Julia in with another comic."

"I want to tell them," Mia said, leaning forward a little, preparatory to getting up.

Boyd shook his head. "Uh-uh. Let them sweat a little. It won't be long, and it'll do them good. It's about time they faced up to the consequences of their actions. They didn't have to raise a row at the club. They could have objected quietly."

"Oh, I don't know. I suppose it was a matter of principle with them—with Julia, anyway."

"Are you implying that my father is *not* a man of principle?" Boyd asked coldly.

"Not at all. Just that I know my mother. She gets very uptight when she thinks an injustice has been done." Mia rose stiffly. "And I'll make my own decisions, thank you. If I want to relieve my mother's anxiety *now*, I'll do it. I don't believe in making the people you love *sweat*, as you so charmingly put it."

Just then a beaming Ron came out of the Captain's office and bustled over to them. He nodded to Julia and Romney. "It's okay. You can go."

Julia thanked him effusively, and Romney gave him a strong, grateful handshake.

Ron waved their thanks aside. "It's nothing. Boyd and I are old friends. Right, old buddy?" He clapped Boyd on the shoulder.

Mia stifled a groan. Was everyone a would-be comic?

Ron swept the four of them with a knowing look. "Besides, we couldn't break up a family."

A considerably chastened Julia and Romney walked out of the police station with Mia and Boyd.

"Maybe you'd better have Romney take you right home, Mom. I'll be there shortly to make you a nice cup of tea, and then you can go to bed."

To Mia's surprise, Julia agreed.

It occurred to Mia as she watched Romney solicitously bundle Julia into his two-seater that she hadn't told her mother she and Boyd were planning to marry. Now was not the time, Mia decided. Suddenly she wondered if there ever would be a time.

They had never sat stiffly apart in the Lamborghini, looking straight ahead, without even a glance in the other's direction.

"Tonight's experience wasn't really a joke," Boyd finally said. "The folks *are* behaving like rebellious teenagers, and it's up to us to keep them in line, or at least out of jail."

"That means playing parent to two *elderly* teenagers."

"That's the size of it. The worst part is that we're not doing it successfully."

That was true, Mia thought. And if they couldn't help their parents lead better lives, how could they expect to control their own teenagers when they had them?

Suddenly the wonderful harmony that she and Boyd enjoyed seemed hollow and empty. It simply didn't hold up under stress. It was obvious to Mia that if she and Boyd couldn't agree on how to handle this facsimile of a domestic situation, they would probably have trouble with the real thing.

Every night for the next week Mia came home from work to an assortment of roasts, fancy fish dishes, vegetables au gratin, homemade ice cream, lemon meringue pies, and fudge—and a long-faced Julia.

"I know it's too much," Julia said apologetically, waving her hands toward a table worthy of Henry the Eighth. "But what am I to do with myself? The Laff-A-Minute's still closed, and Romney has a cold."

Mia eyed all the food. At this rate she'd be the Librarian-Who-Weighed-a-Ton. "How about making chicken soup for Romney?"

"He's got so much, he could can it and open a factory. Chicken rice, chicken vegetable, chicken noodle—"

Mia held a hand up. "Okay, Mom, I get the picture. Isn't this a good time, since the Laff-A-Minute's closed, to find another challenging second career?"

"Oh, the club won't stay closed," Julia said with confidence.

"Oh?" Mia replied, suddenly wary. "Why not?"

"Romney and I have been picketing the district attorney's office. That's how Romney caught his cold."

Mia closed her eyes in disbelief.

"You mean picketing with signs?"

"Why, of course, Mia, how else does one picket? Really, sometimes you seem a little slow."

Mia let her remark pass. "Do you think that was wise, Mom? Romney's down with a cold, and you seem tense and tired."

"I think it will get results. The case is coming up in a week. Romney and I are going to testify in favor of Mr. Baker. In the meanwhile this lets the D.A. know how the public feels about comedy clubs."

Boyd didn't call that evening or the next or the one after that. At first Mia wondered if she was seeing a side of Boyd she hadn't known existed. Perhaps he had an angry, vengeful trait that didn't usually show.

"Do you think Boyd has a mean streak in him?" she asked her mother.

Julia laughed. "Boyd? Not at all. He has the sweetest disposition of any man I've ever met, except your father and Romney."

Mia silently agreed. After another day had passed, she concluded that Boyd didn't want to talk to her. It was his way of calling it quits.

"Boyd hasn't called since the night we got you and Romney out of jail. I think we're finished."

Julia shook her head decisively. "No way. I've seen how he looks at you. He's crazy about you. He's probably afraid to give you Romney's cold."

"Over the phone?" Mia said.

"Well, a phone call would lead to a date, wouldn't it?" Julia replied reasonably. "And I don't suppose you two shake hands when you say good night. A kiss is the surest way to spread a cold virus."

"Hmm." Mia wasn't convinced. She was sure she would never hear from Boyd again, except possibly in a casual way. A sadness crept over her spirit.

Then the phone rang. Mia picked up the receiver. Her heart started pounding in her chest when she heard Boyd's familiar voice.

"Mia?" he said gently. "I don't want you to think I'm angry with you. I've been taking care of Dad, and I caught his cold, and I've felt too rotten to talk."

A wave of relief swept over Mia. Her heartbeat returned to normal, and she relaxed her tense grip on the phone. "That's all right, Boyd. I'm sorry you haven't been feeling well. Anything I can do?"

Boyd cleared his throat. When he spoke again, his voice was cooler and less affectionate. "Well, yes, actually there is. Please stop your mother from carrying that ridiculous picket sign back and forth outside the district attorney's office. Romney threatens to rejoin her as soon as his cold is better, and I can't stop him."

Mia's temper flared. "You can't stop your dad from doing something silly, but you expect me to stop my mother? Isn't that unreasonable?"

"Well, one of us should be able to do something!" Mia could hear the nasal sounds of a bad cold in Boyd's voice. She longed to go to his condo and take care of him. She pictured herself bringing him his meals in bed, rubbing his back, making him comfortable. But the way he was picking on Julia caused her desire to fade quickly.

"You try it first," Mia said. "I'm not interfering with Mom's right as a citizen to protest." She hung up the phone before Boyd could answer and sat there fuming until Julia entered the den.

"That was Boyd," Mia said. "He wants me to stop you from picketing before Romney rejoins you." She looked at her mother suspiciously. "What did your sign say anyway?"

"It was direct and right to the point."

"Yes, Mom, but what point?" Mia asked wearily.

"*I* painted the sign instead of Romney, because I taught art for a while, you know, dear."

Mia waited.

"It said: 'D.A. a dodo. Free the comedy clubs.' "

" 'D.A. a dodo.' I'm sure that went over big in the D.A.'s office."

"It showed public opinion," Julia said stoutly. "But if it distresses you, I won't picket anymore. I don't want Romney going out too soon after his cold anyway.

"Thanks, Mom. I'm not sure Boyd's friend Ron could spring you two again."

The next day when Mia came home from the library, she was met at the door by a beaming Julia.

"I have some very important news," Julia said, hastening Mia inside. "Boyd called."

Mia's heart seemed to stop for a minute.

An anxious frown knitted her mother's brow. "Not about you, dear." Julia averted her eyes from the disappointed look on Mia's face and hurried on.

"The Laff-A-Minute's going to reopen. The D.A. won't need Romney's and my testimony. Ron told Boyd that the charge was thrown out of court when the customer who made the complaint confessed that he had done so maliciously because he had a grudge against the owner, Mr. Baker. The club's liquor license is being restored, and there won't be any fine."

Mia hugged her mother. "That's wonderful news for you and Romney and for Mr. Baker."

Julia stepped back and eyed Mia speculatively. "It was very nice of Boyd to call and tell me. In fact, I wouldn't be surprised if his friend Ron didn't facilitate matters."

Mia shrugged and said coolly, "Boyd's a nice guy. Just because we quarreled doesn't mean he suddenly became a villain."

"What did you quarrel about, Mia? Me and Romney?"

Mia slipped out of her cardigan and threw it on a chair. "In a word, yes. Each of us thought the other should have watched out more for you two."

"As though we were children!" Julia said reproachfully.

Mia didn't answer. She started toward the kitchen, the source of a delicious odor. "What are you cooking, Mom?"

"Beef Stroganoff, and I should be in there now stirring it." She followed Mia into the kitchen and, taking a long-handled wooden spoon, began stirring the beef dish in a heavy iron pot.

"Can I help?" Mia asked.

"You can set the table."

As Mia set out the plates and silverware, Julia said meditatively, "You may not ever have known this, but your dad and I used to quarrel about you when you were a child."

Mia looked up from folding a napkin, surprised. "No, I didn't know."

"Well, it's considered better not to have a child see that her parents disagree about how to handle her. Therefore we waited until you were in bed before having our discussions about you."

Mia was amused. "All this was going on, and I didn't even know it. What did you disagree about?"

"Oh, how late you should be allowed to stay up, how much TV you could watch, whether you should have more responsibilities around the house."

"Who was the strict one and who the lenient?"

"Can't you guess?" Julia said with a teasing smile as she continued to stir the sauce with long, rhythmic strokes.

"You were strict, and Dad was the softie."

Julia nodded. She peered searchingly into the pot. "I think this is about ready."

"How did you end up deciding what I could do or couldn't do? I mean, decisions were made. You and Dad must have reached an agreement."

"We always did eventually. Sometimes your father would give in, sometimes I would. It took a lot of midnight sessions, but I think we managed to guide you through childhood fairly successfully."

"I think you did," Mia agreed. "I can't remember any major traumas in either my childhood or teenage years." In fact, Mia thought, her parents had done a better job with her than she and Boyd had done with Julia and Romney.

Raising children to be happy adults was a tremendous responsibility. Failure could even sour a marriage. Mia thought of people she knew whose teen-agers gave them nothing but trouble. When the couple went out for the evening, they were tense with worry about where their kids really were, who their companions were, and whether they would get home safely.

Sometimes their bitterness at their situation surfaced in recriminations even in the company of friends. Their unhappiness with themselves, with their children, and with each other was palpable.

Mia had felt sorry for them and, with her own happy childhood to look back upon, had been sure nothing of the kind could happen to her.

Now she wasn't so sure.

It might be wise for her and Boyd to put off their marriage. It was a painful thought, but it was better to be cautious than sorry later. The first opportunity she had, she would discuss the idea with Boyd.

Mia thought about her decision during the night and the next day at work in the library. She struggled with the idea, trying to find a way to avoid depriving herself and Boyd of the joy they had anticipated. But she kept returning to the same thought: it was better to wait than be sorry.

That night Jerry Baker called Julia. Mia could hear snatches of her mother's conversation.

"I'll be there tomorrow night, Mr. Baker, bright-eyed and bushy-tailed," Julia said. "And so will Romney." There was a pause, then an excited "Mr. Baker! I'm so flattered I don't know what to say. What am I saying?" Julia screamed. "I'm saying *yes*."

Mia looked up from the book she was reading. "What was that all about, Mom?"

"Mr. Baker offered me a contract. I'm going to be a

headliner at the club, with Romney writing my material, of course." Julia looked around distractedly. "I must tell Romney. It's too important for the phone. I want to see his face."

"I'll drive you over, Mom."

"Would you, dear? I'm so excited. It'd be my luck to have an accident just when things are breaking for me."

Mia took both her mother's hands in hers and looked at her affectionately. "I'm proud of you, Mom. You kept trying till you did it. Even in the face of Boyd's and my opposition."

"It was really what I wanted," Julia said seriously. "I knew it in my bones." She looked down shyly. "Then, too, it brought me close to Romney."

Romney's house was a California Tudor, a large brick and stucco building with gables and Gothic windows. A green lawn rolled majestically past beds of thick ivy to the sidewalk. Exotic bird of paradise plants added splashes of bright orange to the velvety green turf. There were glimpses over a gate of a large garden and patio in the rear.

Mia's heart gave an extra little leap when she saw the sleek black Lamborghini parked in the driveway.

"Terrific!" Julia said. "We can tell Boyd our good news at the same time."

Romney came to the door, with Boyd close behind him. The look on Boyd's face when he saw Mia was one of pure happiness. He took her hands and drew her away from Julia and Romney into a room containing a massive desk and reddish-brown leather armchairs.

"What about the others?" Mia asked.

"What others?" Boyd's voice was husky with emotion. "It's been too long, Mia. I'm sorry I was irritable. It was this damn cold of mine and worry about Romney's turning into pneumonia. But we're both all right now."

Boyd couldn't take his eyes off her face. He was starved for the sight of her, of those big gray limpid eyes, her sweet, shapely mouth, the dimple that came and went as she smiled.

He could tell from the glow in her face, from the subtle perfume of desire her body gave off that she felt the same about him.

Confused by a sudden, unexpected onslaught of love for him, Mia let Boyd pull her down onto a leather sofa. He kissed her for timeless sweet minutes that ended with his tongue nestled inside the warmth of her mouth. Then he began to nuzzle her neck, lifting her dark hair to reach the hidden places his lips loved to touch. Mia closed her eyes, feeling her pulse racing, her body quivering with her need.

Hearing Julia and Romney outside the door, they pulled away. Mia picked a magazine up off the table and pretended to read. Boyd applied himself with meticulous attention to lining up the other magazines so they formed one straight edge.

Mia just had time to whisper, "Mom's got a contract to headline at the Laff-A-Minute. She wanted to tell your dad."

Pausing at the doorway, Romney chuckled. "Takes me back a few years, doesn't it you, Julia?"

Julia laughed. "I miss the squeak of the porch swing."

"And the sound when it stops," Romney said.

"All right, wise guys, enough already," Boyd said. Looking down at Mia, he carefully turned her magazine right side up. He stood and walked over to Julia. "My heartfelt congratulations on your contract." He kissed her on the cheek. "You're in line for them, too, Dad. It was your material."

"Well, thanks, son. I guess we all collaborated." Romney coughed, then gave everyone a huge wink. "Julia and I have something important to tell you kids."

"You're not buying another motorcycle?" Boyd asked.

"No, we're through with that nonsense. But we wanted you to know that we're through with the Zebra Lounge as well. All those stripes were getting to me. I was beginning to walk in straight lines everywhere I went."

"Great!" Boyd exclaimed. "That smoke-filled disco was almost as unsafe for you two as the motorcycle."

Romney's blue eyes lit with a twinkle. "We just wanted to tell you youngsters so you could carry on with your own activities without worrying about us." He put his arm around Julia's slim shoulders. "Come on, Julia. We've got to work up some new routines for you, befitting your stature as a headliner at the Laff-A-Minute."

When the door closed gently behind the older couple, Boyd turned to Mia with a wry grin on his face. "We're getting there. First we got rid of the motorcycle. Now they're giving up the Zebra Lounge."

"But they still stay up until all hours at the comedy club."

"Maybe we'd better just accept that," Boyd said softly, "and go ahead with our own lives, as Dad suggested." He took a step toward Mia, his arms out to embrace her.

Mia backed away. She had to tell him the decision she had reached. If she waited and felt the familiar contours of his body pressed against hers, the wild-fire sweep of his lips across her face and throat, she would lose her resolve.

Her hands in front of her, as if to keep him away, Mia said, "Boyd, there's something I have to tell you."

Boyd lifted his dark brows. "This seems to be a day for announcements. Are you trying to tell me that we won't be going to the Zebra Lounge anymore either?"

Mia motioned to the leather sofa. "I think we should sit down. We may have some discussing to do."

Boyd shot her a speculative look, then sat down beside her at the distance her outspread hand indicated he should take.

Mia looked square into his face. She was going to do this right.

"I think we should postpone getting married for a while. I think we need to give it some more thought."

Boyd looked concerned. "Why, for heaven's sake? Don't you love me anymore?"

Mia glanced away. She loved him with every inch of her being. Her heart was pounding with her fear of losing him. Her body trembled with need.

"In a way, that's beside the point," Mia said gently.

"*Love* is beside the point in marriage?" Boyd's tone was lightly sarcastic.

"Children are very important to me, Boyd. I couldn't bear to have kids and not bring them up right. Just think how miserable it must be to have children you've nurtured for years turn out to be unhappy adults."

"I entirely agree," Boyd said earnestly. "But what makes you think our kids would turn out like that?"

"Look at our parents! We certainly haven't succeeded in getting them out of the comedy business. Quite the opposite! Mom's got a contract now, and Romney's writing all her material. We couldn't even agree on how to handle them, so what are we going to do—fight with each other *and* our kids as they go through adolescence?"

Boyd remained silent a long time. "I see your point," he said finally. "I love you, Mia, and I know you still love me somewhere beneath it all, but marriage is a serious step. I'm not planning on marrying and then divorcing if things don't work out." His voice took on a note of panic. "We'll still see each other, though, won't we?"

Mia smiled and put her hand out to him. "I still haven't seen those etchings of yours."

Nine

Frances slapped a sheet of paper on the counter in front of Mia, pinning it down with her index finger. "Now, that's something I would really like to go to."

Mia glanced down at the flier. It announced in big black letters a librarians' convention in Palm Springs that coming weekend.

"Then why don't you?" Mia asked.

Frances shook her head. "Can't. I've got relatives coming from Iowa. Besides, this is the last notice. I should have registered already to get in. Palm Springs!" Frances sighed. "Everyone will want to go."

"What happened to the first notices?" Mia asked.

"I gave them to you. You just didn't pay attention."

That was undoubtedly true, Mia thought. Two weeks had passed since she and Boyd had made the decision to delay their marriage, and she had been in a state of doubt and uncertainty ever since. They had seen each other almost every night but had concluded each evening with a good night kiss at her door.

The sexual tension between them crackled when they were together, but by tacit agreement they did nothing about it. Mia was sure that if they went to bed together, they would end up marrying as soon as possible. They wanted each other on a permanent basis. Lovemaking would be the spark to ignite the flames they had banked inside them.

Perhaps it wasn't such a good idea to continue dating, Mia thought. One of them might crack under the prolonged strain and call the whole relationship off. A few days away from each other would ease the tension.

Mia kept the flier in front of her all morning as she checked out books. The convention began Friday evening and ended Sunday at noon. There might have been a cancellation. She glanced at the big clock on the wall. It was worth a try.

There had been a cancellation, she was informed by the convention organizer in Los Angeles. Mia could pay when she registered.

"I'll get back to you," Mia said. "First I have to see if I can get Saturday off."

Frances was standing by the telephone. "Why don't you take Monday and Tuesday off too," she proposed. "It's been a long time since you've had a vacation, and frankly you look a little peaked."

Five days away from Boyd! Was it a good idea? Mia wondered. How much fun could she have in Palm Springs alone?

Upon reflection, Mia realized that she wouldn't be completely alone. Some of the other librarians would probably stay over too.

A quiet time by herself was just what she needed to think about the future. The five days would be a testing time to see how she and Boyd bore separation.

After two more phone calls—to her supervisor and to the Palm Springs hotel—all arrangements were made.

"Thanks for the suggestion, Frances. I'll be gone through Tuesday. You'll be working with a substitute librarian named Agnes Hooper. I know her. She's a very pleasant person to work with."

"Oh, I'm sure we'll get along just fine. You may come back and find all the books in the wrong places, but what the heck, a library is a moveable feast."

That evening after work Mia drove to a department store in a nearby shopping mall and bought a new swimsuit. Palm Springs was undoubtedly full of stores that featured pool attire, but they might be expensive. The suit was a nylon and lycra tank with the look of black lace. It had the thinnest of spaghetti straps and a bow at the small of the back. Pretty sexy for a librarian, Mia acknowledged with a smile, but she would get her money's worth out of the swimsuit this summer.

She waited until the last possible moment to call Boyd. She didn't want to quarrel about their parents again, nor did she want him to sweet-talk her into not going to Palm Springs.

As the phone rang in his condo, she pictured the scene. He might have lit the fire. The flames would be dancing behind the glass doors while he sat on the couch, reading or watching TV.

Suddenly it all seemed so pointless and lonely.

Boyd all alone in his apartment; she alone in her house, with Julia gone almost all the time.

When he answered the phone, she was tempted to say "Let's not wait, Boyd. Let's just go ahead and get married now."

But as the shrill sound ripped away at the silence, Mia thought, what if he said no and insisted on waiting?

Just then the phone was picked up. She could hear somebody's labored breathing.

"Aha!" Mia joked. "A heavy breather."

"I was just getting out of the elevator," Boyd answered. "I thought it might be you, so I ran for the phone. Do you want to make plans for tonight?"

The boyish eagerness in his voice made Mia feel bad about what she was going to tell him. "Not tonight, Boyd," she said. "Maybe next Wednesday."

"How come not till Wednesday? What about the weekend?"

"I'll be in Palm Springs. There's a librarians' convention there. I'll be at the Desert Breeze Hotel, if you want to call."

"Oh sure, Mia." Boyd sounded totally deflated. "Have a good time, and I'll be talking to you."

Boyd slipped a frozen dinner into the microwave and stood staring down at the lighted interior. Nobody *had* to go to a convention. Mia was going to Palm Springs to get away from the inflammable situation between them.

Waiting was the hardest thing anyone could do. It was putting an intolerable strain on his relationship with Mia. The delights of a married life together were always in view but out of reach, like forbidden fruit.

Whereas formerly they had been easy with each other, now they seemed always to be on guard, afraid of saying the wrong thing and starting another quarrel. They used to touch each other frequently in signs of love and mutual affection. Now they never did. It was as if they might explode if they touched.

The microwave buzzer sounded. Boyd took his dinner out and ate it standing up at the kitchen counter.

Halfway through he put his fork down. The food was so tasteless, it was hard to tell the dinner from the cardboard container. But that wasn't what was bothering him.

He was a man of action, accustomed to making decisions and following through on them. This passive waiting around to see what Julia and Romney would do and what would develop in his relationship with Mia was driving him up the wall.

But it wasn't true, Boyd reflected as he put the kettle on for a cup of instant coffee, that any decision, even a wrong one, was better than no decision. He prided himself on always making the *right* decision. All it took was a little more thought.

Well, he had all the time in the world, Boyd decided, spooning some instant coffee into a mug. *He* wasn't going anywhere tonight.

At nine o'clock Saturday morning, Mia went to the first of the workshops she had signed up for the night before—a seminar on imaginative literature for children. She lunched on the patio of a colorful

Mexican restaurant with a librarian from Fresno and another from Sacramento. There would be time for a dip in the pool before the afternoon seminars began.

It was going to be a *very* educational weekend, Mia thought, stifling a yawn while her luncheon companions divided the check three ways.

On the way back to the hotel Mia found her gaze drifting to couples strolling along Palm Canyon Drive. They looked so happy with their arms around each other's waists that Mia felt a pang of longing for Boyd.

She stopped at the desk to see if there were any messages. But her key box was empty. Disappointed, she went to her room and changed into her swimsuit. She hadn't really expected a phone call from Boyd, but she wished fervently that there had been one.

The pool was almost empty. Mia swam laps until she was tired out. The exercise was invigorating and took her mind off Boyd. Then she lay in the sun long enough to get the beige Palm Springs look, but not so long as to get sunburned.

Still, the sun and the exercise had made her sleepy, and she nodded off during the afternoon at a lecture on the use of computers in the library.

Checking for telephone messages had gotten to be almost a compulsion. Boyd knew where she was staying. If he cared for her, why didn't he call? Mia asked herself.

Because, dummy, her alternate self answered, you're the one who left, and you're the one who wanted to postpone the marriage. He probably figures it's all over and has started dating somebody else.

When Mia saw the white telephone slip in her box, her heart leaped. But to forestall disappointment, she told herself it was probably Julia or one of the other librarians at the convention.

Mia waited patiently for a room clerk to hand her the slip of paper. She opened it with trembling fingers. Then she had all she could do not to shout with joy right there in the hotel lobby.

The paper bore Boyd's name and phone number.

Mia's impulse was to run to the nearest phone. Her glance fell on the tables around the pool, one of which held a slim white telephone that had probably just been used by a movie mogul.

Mia couldn't even wait to get to her room. She left the lobby by the glass patio doors and headed for the phone. She had no sooner given the long-distance operator her room number than she regretted it. The pool, she now saw, was full of children playing noisily. The dry desert air seemed to magnify the voices of the couples at the tables around her.

When she heard Boyd's warm, mellow voice, all her worries and fears vanished.

"I got your message," she said almost shyly. Then she laughed. "That's silly, isn't it? Of course I got your message. That's why I'm calling."

Someone let out an especially loud whoop of exuberance in the background.

"Sounds as though you're having a good time," Boyd said sourly.

"I'm poolside. That's the reason for all the noise."

"Poolside! Didn't they give you a room?"

Mia laughed again, a ripple of sheer delight. "I was in a hurry," she explained.

His voice dropped to the low, sexy purr Mia loved. "So am I. I miss you. Can I come down and see you? How about a late dinner together, tonight?"

"Terrific, except that I don't think you'll be able to get accommodations. The town's full."

"Don't worry about that. I have access to a villa."

"I forgot you were in real estate," Mia said.

"It's a handy profession sometimes. The soonest I can get down there is eight o'clock. Is it all right if I pick you up at eight-thirty?"

"Fine. I'll be ready."

Cheeks flushed, heart beating fast and happily, Mia hung up the phone.

It was a well-known fact that hotel dress shops were the most expensive places anywhere to buy clothes, but Mia didn't care. She'd spend six month's salary just to see that special light in Boyd's eyes when she wore something he liked.

"A sexy little black dress," she told the deeply tanned, blond saleswoman.

Several were brought out for Mia's inspection. She didn't look at the price tags until she had them in the dressing room, then she almost fainted.

The saleswoman knocked on the door. "Here's a little number that we've marked down because it's winter stock, and we're showing our spring collection now."

Summer, winter, autumn, spring. What difference did the season make in Palm Springs?

The dress had a short-sleeved sequin-covered top and a silk tulip skirt, all in black.

"It's a charming dinner dress," the saleswoman said.

This time Mia looked at the price tag. "The price is an improvement," she said with a wry smile.

The blonde smiled back at her. "Try it on. I think it'll look wonderful on you."

It was a perfect fit. The sequins covered her breasts discreetly, at the same time giving a hint of the shapely fullness beneath. The skirt reached her knees and clung to her rounded hips.

Mia was ecstatic as she paid for the dress. After she had hung it in the closet of her room, she went to the beauty salon for "the works."

At eight-thirty there was a soft knock at her door, and she opened it to Boyd.

"Wow! What a knockout! This must be Mia Taylor's room."

"No, it isn't." Mia pretended to look him over. "But come in anyway."

Boyd looked utterly handsome in a navy suit.

"You're beautiful, Mia." He put his hand out and laughed. "You look so gorgeous, I'm afraid to touch you."

"Touch me," Mia replied softly, invitingly.

With a low groan, he crushed her in his arms and kissed her with a hunger she had never felt in him before. "I've missed you so. Things had gotten so strained between us, I was afraid when I called you would tell me not to come."

"I kept looking in my box for a message. When I finally saw one, I was terrified that it might not be from you," Mia said against his shoulder.

"We were fools," Boyd said bitterly, "but we'll have to talk about that later. We've got to go. Edwin's is one restaurant where you don't come late—not if you still want your table."

They drove to the restaurant under an onyx sky. In the dry desert air, the stars seemed bright and close. A warm wind laved them with the sweet scent of night-blooming jasmine.

"Everything seems so magical, so exotic," Mia said.

"Palm Springs at night is like that," Boyd agreed as he turned into the parking lot of the restaurant. "The oasis was built on an Indian burial ground, and it's said that the spirits walk at night. That's hard to believe around these expensive hotels and estates. But you only have to drive for five minutes to find yourself in the desert, where it isn't hard to believe."

Edwin was a short, plump man weighed down by a huge Indian-made turquoise and silver necklace. His stubby fingers were adorned with turquoise rings, and his watchband was made of turquoise also. Edwin greeted everyone personally, making them feel like his guests rather than customers.

The dining room combined elegance with comfort. Crystal chandeliers shed soft light. The napery, crystal, and silverware were beyond reproach. Exotic desert flowers adorned the tables, which were set far apart so that each diner had a sense of privacy.

"What do you think?" Boyd asked, beaming with pride, his vibrant gaze on her face.

"It's beautiful!" Mia answered enthusiastically.

"Wait till you taste the food. Edwin stole one of the best chefs in France from a three-star Paris restaurant."

They ended up feasting on Dungeness crab legs Florentine as an appetizer, cucumber glacé, a salad of limestone lettuce with baby shrimp, and roasted quail with grapes as an entrée. They had a chocolate charlotte for dessert with a demitasse served in thin white china cups.

When they finally finished, Mia said, "I'll never have to eat again. Never!"

"I'll cook for you tomorrow night. I'll grill steaks on our patio."

"*Our* patio?"

Boyd lowered his voice to a seductive murmur. "I want to show you my villa."

"Don't tell me you moved your etchings down from San Ramon!"

"This place comes complete with everything, including etchings."

They drove back through the dark night to Palm Canyon Drive and turned off on a street called Jacaranda Road. The narrow street was lined with flowering lavender-blossomed Jacaranda trees and wound around the base of Mount San Jacinto.

Boyd pulled up to a high wall beyond which loomed the tops of tall palms. He used a plastic card to open a gate in the wall and drove up to a large white stuccoed bungalow.

"This is it," Boyd said. "The wall allows for nude sunbathing. No one can look in. We have our own private pool and Jacuzzi, and our own tennis court."

"Wow! Talk about luxury."

"Wait until you see the inside," Boyd boasted. He led her proudly through the villa. "Three bedrooms, each with its own private bath—the master bedroom has a sunken bath—a living room with a fireplace, stereo system, and TV. A fully equipped kitchen." He flipped on the lights, and an ultramodern, gleaming kitchen came into view.

The entire apartment was filled with roses of various shades, from a rich coppery-gold to deep crimson. Their sweet scent perfumed the air.

"Boyd, I'm impressed," Mia said as he took her hand and led her back into the living room. "It's a lovely place, but what do you plan to do with all this space?"

"I own it, Mia," Boyd said quietly. "The whole complex of condos, tennis courts, and a swimming pool. It's called Siesta Villas. This could be our winter vacation home. The bedrooms could be for the kids." He gripped her hands and looked earnestly into her face. "We were foolish to put our love at risk for the sake of an impossible ideal. No one's perfect. Why should we expect to be perfect marriage partners or perfect parents?"

Mia stared down at his strong, supple hands. "You're right, and it was all my fault, because I started it. I was the one who wanted to wait."

"It was no one's fault, Mia. We were both equally foolish. I think the shock of seeing Julia and Romney in jail threw us both into a tailspin." Boyd began to laugh. "Imagine that little firebrand, Julia, picketing the D.A.'s office."

"I know," Mia said affectionately. "Mom's irrepressible. She needs someone solid like your dad to steady her. But really, I don't think we did a bad job bringing them up."

"Neither do I. At least they're not sitting home vegetating. They're out enjoying life."

"Obviously living it to the full, delighting in each other and in every day."

"That takes faith and courage, Mia. It means taking risks." Boyd's voice deepened. "How do you feel about risking your future with me? I love you, and I want us to spend the rest of our lives together."

"At the moment I'm tempted to say that there'd be no risk involved because I love you too. But that's not true. Life's a risky proposition always, but at least we'd be facing it together."

She reached up and, winding her arms around Boyd's neck, kissed him passionately. All the love Mia had bottled up for months burst out and flowed through her into the kiss as she clung tightly to Boyd.

"I've wanted you for so long," Boyd murmured. He moved his thumb slowly across her shoulder and up her neck. His thumb felt faintly rough against her skin, branding it with heat. An answering warmth sprang up deep in Mia's abdomen. She leaned back and stretched like a cat, offering her throat to his touch.

Boyd's hand spread out over her neck and shoulders. He pressed his lips to her throat. His lips were soft and velvety. The kiss shot through Mia like a jolt of electricity.

"Oh, Boyd," she murmured in a haunting whisper, "what if we hadn't made up?"

"We would have," he answered confidently. "We could never have stayed away from each other."

Mia felt reassured.

Boyd kissed her again, opening her lips to his with his tongue. Mia shivered at the familiar delight and melted against him.

Boyd groaned and his arms slid around her. It had been so long since he had felt her softness against him. For days and days his body had ached to feel her again.

His kiss was filled with passion, and Mia responded with equal hunger. Boyd felt her warm breath in his mouth, against his face. His hands roamed her body. Her fingers dug into the silk of his sport shirt.

Mia pressed up against him, her breasts flattening against his chest. He ran his hands over the curve of her derriere and down her shapely thighs, bunching up the thin material of her dress, aware of nothing but the need to feel her skin beneath his fingertips. His long fingers slid up the smooth silkiness of her hose and onto the flesh above, and his hand trembled.

Gently he picked Mia up and carried her to the immense, king-sized bed, where he undressed her and quickly shed his own clothes. He rolled back the rose-colored coverlet and placed her between the fine cotton sheets.

Bending over her, he said poignantly, "I was afraid at times it would never come to this." Then his sparkling blue eyes turned suddenly stern. He added, "Remember, I'm talking marriage, woman. Your intentions toward me are honorable, aren't they?"

Mia threw her arms up behind her head and smiled lazily. "Oh, I don't know, for the moment I feel more like a kept woman. A luxurious villa, flowers, and my own swimming pool. It sure beats the library."

Boyd laughed. "I don't know what *that* does to my ego—being compared to the San Ramon Community Library." He lowered his voice to a sexy growl. "But I know what *this* does." Wrapping his arms around her, Boyd raised Mia to him as his mouth came down over hers. He crushed her soft breasts against the hard planes of his chest and held her hips tight against his.

Mia shivered and made a tiny wild sound as her teeth nibbled at his lips. She bit them gently, then soothed the spot with her tongue. She ran her hands up and down his long, supple back, delighting in the strength of his muscles.

Boyd let her fall back onto the bed and brushed her soft neck with his fingertips. "You don't get this kind of love in libraries, lady," he said jokingly.

"Oh yeah? You should have seen what went on in college."

Boyd wove a chain of kisses around Mia's earlobe, then dropped his lips to the throbbing pulse in her neck. Mia closed her eyes in delight and stretched sensuously on the bed.

Boyd feasted his eyes on Mia's creamy, rose-peaked breasts. He feathered his palm over one breast until the peak hardened further and pressed eagerly against his hand. Mia watched his eyes darken to the hues of an ocean storm.

"Boyd!" Mia whispered urgently. "Please, darling, now!" She was a volcano of desire, throbbing from her kiss-swollen lips to the very heart of her femininity.

She lifted her hips to receive his gentle penetrating thrust. Moaning with joy, she opened to receive him. As he began to move inside her, she met each of his slow, plunging strokes lovingly.

Together they created their own world, a universe of love made by a man and a woman who cared for each other. Together they soared from one peak of ecstasy to an ever-higher one. Finally, suspended on the very pinnacle of bliss, they called each other's name, testifying to their love.

Afterward they lay silently together, legs entwined, fingers laced, as if they couldn't bear to separate. Sated, content, they fell asleep, their senses adrift on the perfume of night-blooming jasmine and roses.

They slept late the next day. Boyd persuaded Mia to skip the farewell luncheon at the convention.

"But I'll have to go to the hotel and get my clothes, and check out."

"I'll do that for you so you won't be detained by one of your librarian friends."

"Pack my suitcase?" Mia said, surprised.

Boyd shrugged. "If you think you're going to need clothes."

While Boyd was gone, Mia stretched out on a chaise longue on the patio.

Waves of joy rippled through her as she thought of the wonderful night she had spent with Boyd. It gave her a warm, exciting feeling to know that there would be many more such nights, passed in the security of a loving, caring marriage.

Gradually Mia felt herself drifting off into sleep. She didn't hear the patio gate open, didn't smell the heady scent of orange trees and oleander, as the sun-drenched warm air drugged her senses.

Boyd saw Mia immediately, lying on the chaise loungue. Her face was turned toward him, her lips curved up in a happy smile. He looked at her body— the small but well-set shoulders, the satiny skin of her back, her long, elegant legs.

His blue eyes crinkling with love and amusement,

Boyd sat down lightly on the chaise and ran one finger down Mia's straight spine.

"Ooh, that feels lovely. Do it again," Mia said from between her folded arms.

"You were supposed to be asleep."

"I was until you sat down."

"How did you know it was me?" Boyd asked. "It could have been Jack the Ripper."

"It wouldn't have mattered. Poor old Jack would have been so enervated by all this sun and heat, he couldn't have ripped open a pack of cigarettes."

Boyd ran his hand down Mia's smooth back. "You look done on this side. Suppose I turn you over."

He put his hands around her waist and gently lifted her a little before setting her down on her back.

"You look even better on this side."

"I think you're a breast man," Mia murmured contentedly.

"Certainly not a *spine* man," Boyd retorted as he bent his head, pulled down the top of her bathing suit, and teased one nipple, then the other with the tip of his tongue.

"Or spineless, thank heaven."

It felt so good to be in Boyd's arms, to breathe in his clean, slightly sweaty scent. And when his hand swooped across her firm little belly, a hot sweet fire began to burn inside her. The touch of his hands on her hips and thighs and the place where she longed for him the most was sweet agony.

He stood up and, gazing down at her with love and admiration, he took off his blue polo shirt and tan slacks.

With her heart overflowing with happiness, Mia

suddenly became mischievous. As Boyd reached for her, she jumped up, eluding his grasp, and ran to the pool.

Laughing at him over her shoulder, Mia called out, "Last one in's a rotten egg!"

She cleaved the water in a neat dive and felt its coolness against her skin. Then she settled into a fast-paced crawl until Boyd grabbed her ankle and held her up in the water.

"You know what happens to uncooperative kept women?" Boyd said.

Mia's eyes sparkled. "They get dunked?"

"Worse," Boyd muttered.

Standing in the shallow water and holding her, his hands slippery yet tight under her breasts, Boyd kissed her long and hard. Her lips parted under the longed-for embrace, and his tongue, velvety and moist, played exciting games with hers. Then, lifting her in his arms, he carried Mia the few steps to the Jacuzzi.

"Umm, delicious," Mia said, as the jets of warm water struck her body.

"Me or the water?"

She pushed a lock of thick brown hair off his forehead and kissed him there. She ran her finger down his strong nose and across his lips. How very precious his face was to her, she realized.

He moved his hands down her slick back removing her suit as he went and raised her out of the water, holding her suspended in his strong arms. His warm mouth sought her navel, the tongue flicking and probing, moving with deliberate, sensual provocation down her smooth belly.

Then he slowly lowered her into the warm water

and ran his lips along the smooth elegant line of her slender neck, stopping only when he reached her erect, pretty pink nipples. He played with each one, blowing miniature jets of warm water onto them.

"Do you like that?" he asked huskily.

"Umm. Who needs a Jacuzzi with you around?"

Boyd half-closed his eyes in a smile. He turned her a little and pulled her onto his lap. His caresses became urgent, his hands seeking her most sensitive, hidden places while his mouth and lips ravished her with hot, moist kisses.

Passion flamed up in her like a towering inferno. The unbearably sweet agony couldn't continue. She had to end it.

"Take me, Boyd. I'm completely yours. Take me now." She forced herself down onto him and watched with delight as his sapphire-blue eyes deepened with love and desire. With each passionate thrust, she felt herself propelled further and further into a magical world of total, glorious sensation, her final release a shower of shooting stars.

They frolicked in the Jacuzzi for a while, then he lifted her out of the warm water and carried her into the bath adjoining the master bedroom. Eyeing the sunken tub, he said, "We'll have to try that sometime."

He wound a huge snow-white bath sheet around both of them and patted them both dry. Wrapping Mia in it, he carried her into the bedroom and laid her tenderly on the bed. Then he turned to go.

"Where are you going?"

"Be right back," he said mysteriously. Boyd returned a minute later, carrying a large box wrapped in gold foil. "Open it. It's for you."

Mia untied the gold ribbon and lifted the cover.

Inside was a froth of black lace topped by a strand of pearls.

"It's my kept woman outfit!" she exclaimed.

"Right," Boyd said. "What every kept woman needs. Try it on."

Mia laughed. She got out of bed and donned the lacy see-through black negligee. "It fits."

"I'll say it does," Boyd muttered. "Here, let me put the pearls on for you."

He stood behind her and fastened the strand around her neck, then he lifted the necklace and left a trail of kisses where the pearls had been. He turned her around and kissed her softly on the lips. He led her back to the bed.

Later, much later, Boyd said, "This is paradise. I wish we didn't have to go back."

"I know, darling," Mia said, stretching out sensuously beside him in the immense bed. "But just think how happy the folks will be when we tell them the good news."

"You know, the last few days have been the first time in months I haven't thought of Julia and Romney." Boyd reached out an arm for her and pulled her close. "See what you do for me?"

"Hmm," Mia answered, as his hand drifted languidly down the side of her hip. A frown creased her brow. "I wonder what those merry pranksters are up to now?" As Boyd's hand did even more delightful things to her, the frown vanished. Like Scarlett O'Hara, she'd think of Julia and Romney tomorrow.

Ten

Mia and Boyd stayed at the villa until the last possible minute. On their last night, Boyd barbecued steaks on the patio for an early supper. Mia baked two russet-brown potatoes and made a green salad.

They worked side by side in matching butcher-type aprons. "Pass me the steak sauce, love," Boyd said. As he took the bottle from her hand, Mia felt her fingers tingle. Even now, after so many nights and days of passionate, completely fulfilling love-making, he could still excite her with just a touch.

"Do you have any tinfoil to wrap the potatoes in?" Mia asked.

Boyd grinned. "Come and get it." He pointed to the cupboard between the refrigerator and the corner he was working in.

"You could hand it to me," Mia said humorously.

Boyd shook his head. "Uh-uh. I'm in the steak, not the baked potato, department. We don't want to blur the lines of authority here, do we?"

"Absolutely not," Mia said with mock horror. "I've been worried about that."

Mia loved Boyd's slightly crooked grin. He gave her a knowing, intimate look that made Mia feel intensely loved and cared about.

She took a few steps forward, opened the cabinet door, and reached up. She could feel her breasts, under a new pale blue crocheted bikini, stretch upward with the movement. Then Boyd's hands were around her waist. He kissed her long and hard on the lips. At the same time his hands crept up under the big white apron and cuddled her straining breasts.

When he released her lips, Mia said, "I hate to leave this place, Boyd. It's been an absolute paradise."

"I know," Boyd murmured, his lips pressed against her smooth dark hair. "Where else can you get up in the morning and see an orange-colored sun rise over snow-capped mountains? But we'll be back, hon, right after the wedding."

"I can hardly wait," Mia said in a breathy voice, winding her arms around Boyd's neck.

An hour or so later Mia lay with her head against Boyd's chest. "What were we doing before? I forget."

"Making an early supper." He slapped her lightly on the rump. "You're irresistible, but we'd better get up and do something about those steaks and potatoes."

It was too hot to eat outside, so they carried their plates with the reheated steaks sizzling on them into the cool dining room.

Looking up from his salad, Boyd said, disappointed, "No croutons."

"You kept me too busy, darling," Mia answered.

Then it was time to pack and lock up the villa and start the two-hour drive home.

As the Lamborghini exited the freeway on the San Ramon off-ramp, Boyd glanced at his watch. "It's late enough. I'll bet the folks are at the Laff-A-Minute. Want to take a chance and go see?"

"Great thinking!," Mia replied.

A few minutes later, as Boyd opened the car door in front of the comedy club, Mia whispered in a voice hushed with awe, "I don't believe this. You can hear the laughter all the way out here."

"Let's hurry up and see who's wowing them. I hope it's Julia."

They had come a long way, Mia reflected, from the day Boyd had referred contemptuously to her mother as "the stand-up comic." Looking back, she thought she had fallen in love with him then, even under those unpropitious circumstances. It seemed as though she had always been in love with Boyd. There was a sureness, an inevitability about her feelings for him that was enormously reassuring.

They entered the Laff-A-Minute just in time to see Julia taking her bows to tremendous applause. Finally she held up her hand for silence. "I want to introduce the man who wrote my wonderful material. My fiancé, Romney Baxter."

"Fiancé!" Mia exclaimed, turning to Boyd.

Boyd grinned. "Looks like it'll be a double wedding."

Romney seemed to hang back bashfully, but when the clapping settled into a steady beat, he got up from the table and climbed onto the stage.

"When's the wedding?" someone in the audience called out.

"Good for you seniors!" another person chimed in.

Romney got very red. Julia looked at him affectionately. The applause continued until, with a friendly wave, Julia led the way off the stage.

Mia and Boyd had seated themselves at Romney's table, then got up to hug and congratulate their parents. When all four sat down again, Boyd glanced at Mia who nodded and smiled.

"How about making it a double wedding, folks?" Boyd asked.

Everybody had to get up again for more hugs, congratulations, and, on the part of Mia and Julia, some kisses.

Julia looked speculatively at the stage.

"Mom! Don't you dare do it!" Mia warned.

Julia shrugged good-humoredly and sat down. "I thought the audience might like to know."

"They will—later," Mia assured her.

"The next question," Romney said, "is when."

"And where," Mia said happily.

"And how big," Julia said.

Mia and Boyd wanted the wedding kept small; but Julia and Romney said no, that wouldn't be fair to all their friends and relatives. So they all agreed on a big wedding.

"I'd love a home wedding," Mia said. "I think it's so much more intimate and friendly. But our house is too small."

"No problem. We'll use my house," Romney said.

"We *could* have the reception in the Laff-A-Minute," Julia proposed tentatively.

But Boyd firmly nixed the idea. "Too commercial." He looked around at the grimy walls and scuffed floor. "Among other things," he added, rolling his eyes. "Dad's house would be fine. What do you think, Mia?"

"I'm for it. Mom?"

"Absolutely." Julia's hazel eyes sparkled with enthusiasm. "How about a *garden* wedding, Mia? We'll wear big hats and have a tent set up."

"How about the weather?" Boyd asked.

"We'll have a canopy for the ceremony and a tent for the reception."

"Capital idea," Romney said heartily. "There's plenty of room. I have a pretty rose garden and lots of other flowers. It's a great place for a wedding. There's even room to install a dance floor for the occasion."

Everyone agreed that a garden wedding would be ideal and that it should be held as soon as possible. Julia had gotten a week off from Mr. Baker for her honeymoon, and Mia could hardly wait to return to Boyd's villa in Palm Springs.

"Are you sure you don't want to go to Hawaii, darling?" he asked. "Europe? Somewhere else?"

"Why exchange one paradise for another?"

Julia and Romney wouldn't tell where they were going, but Mia guessed it was to the mountain cabin.

Wedding gifts for both bridal couples began pouring into the Taylors' house. The phone rang constantly with questions from the florist, the caterer, and the leader of the dance band.

Everything had to match in a double wedding, and choosing a wedding dress that would suit both Julia and Mia took a long time. They finally decided on sophisticated but informal off-white gowns to suit their slender figures.

"I never had a wedding," Julia confided to Mia. "Your father and I eloped and got married in city hall. We had the blessings of both sets of parents. My dad had just lost a lot of money, and we were trying to spare him the expense of a wedding. So now I want a beautiful traditional wedding for both of us."

Amid all the excitement of bridal showers and parties, Mia remained calm. All she cared about was being married to Boyd. She wanted every bond—emotional, spiritual, legal—that marriage implied. She wanted to be linked to Boyd forever. If she had to accomplish her goal by having a big wedding instead of a small one; with music and flowers or without; in a white dress or a jumpsuit, it didn't matter to her.

Boyd was as impatient as Mia. "We should have slipped away and got married by ourselves," he grumbled.

"The idea of a double wedding really does please Julia and Romney," Mia pointed out.

"It's driving me nuts, especially as I never see you alone these days."

Mia smiled impishly at him. "Do you mean days or nights?"

"Just wait till we get to Palm Springs," Boyd warned. "Then you'll find out."

Finally the big day arrived. "I know I'm not losing a daughter, I'm gaining a son," Julia said, sniffing a little, "but even so I'll miss you, Mia."

"But you're also gaining a husband, Mom."

Julia brightened up. "Well, that's true. And a wonderful one at that. Romney's so reliable. Not that your father wasn't," Julia hastened to add.

"I know what you mean. Romney was always there for you at the comedy club, night after night. Actually, Boyd takes after his father. He's a man you can depend upon."

"*I* think that's almost the most important quality a person can have."

"So do I," Mia agreed, thinking of Gary. With no effort at all she banished thoughts of Gary. Nothing was going to mar the happiness of the day.

And nothing did. The sky was a cloudless California blue; the weather warm enough for garden attire without even the addition of a sweater. The brides walked with each other down a garden path to the strains of Mendelssohn's wedding march while their grooms, beaming with happiness, waited for them at the altar.

The reception afterward was a cold buffet luncheon served in the garden. Julia had put herself in charge of arrangements with the caterer. There was a fish mousse, a pasta salad, a mixed shellfish salad with a creamy dill dressing, chicken salad with capers, and warm little seed rolls.

Mia and Boyd received the good wishes of the wedding guests for what seemed to them like hours.

Finally Boyd said through clenched teeth, "*When* can we leave?"

"Soon, darling. I promised to hold the fort while Julia and Romney made their getaway first."

Their gazes locked in a long, tender glance. "I love you," Boyd said.

"I know," Mia answered, glowing.

"And if we ever get out of this damn reception, I'm *really* going to prove it to you."

Someone whispered to Mia, "It's time to cut the cake."

When the band swung into "The Blue Danube," Boyd swept Mia into his arms and waltzed with her.

"Remember?" he whispered against her hair.

Mia smiled and nodded. "The saltwater taffy, the carousel, the brass ring." She held her left hand out. A big emerald-cut diamond engagement ring and an old-fashioned gold wedding band adorned her fourth finger. "I would have married you with the brass ring," Mia said lovingly.

Romney and Julia joined them on the dance floor. "I wish they'd play a little rock and roll," Julia said.

There was no urgency in Mia and Boyd's lovemaking that night. Boyd was as gentle yet passionate as any bridegroom could be. They savored each other with lingering abandon. They both knew their love was for all time.

Mia awakened the next morning to an empty bed and the hot golden desert sun streaming into the room. She stretched luxuriously, remembering the pleasures of the night, when Boyd returned. He had put on his pajama bottoms, but above them his chest hair was a nest of soft curls.

He held up a newspaper, his sapphire-blue eyes gleaming with tenderness. "The morning paper is delivered to the door, when I order it ahead of time. This might interest you." He handed the paper, opened to an inside section, to Mia.

With her quick librarian's eye, Mia read the title of

the column, "Southland Social News," recognized the picture of Julia dancing in Romney's arms, and went on to the gushing description of the wedding of famous stand-up comic, Julia Taylor, to Romney Baxter. The columnist also mentioned, in passing, that it had been a double wedding with Julia's daughter, Mia, and Romney's son, Boyd.

Mia handed the paper back to Boyd with a laugh. "Well, I guess that puts *us* in our place, doesn't it?"

Boyd got into bed beside Mia. "Just imagine, we might not even have met if it hadn't been for your mother, the stand-up comic, and my dad, the comedy writer."

He put one golden, tanned arm out and tucked her close to his side. Mia snuggled against him with a contented sigh. "We learned something from them, didn't we, darling?"

"You bet. We learned how to take a chance on love instead of looking for perfection."

Mia wound her arms around Boyd's waist and gave him a little love-bite on the shoulder. "I don't see you as a *chance*," she said, "but an opportunity."

"Let's be specific here," Boyd said with mock roughness. "An opportunity for what?"

"Umm." Mia raised herself on her elbow. She had intended to play with him, to pepper his face with tiny explosive, arousing kisses, but her mood suddenly turned serious. She looked deep into his eyes. "To love each other for the rest of our lives. Until we're older than Julia and Romney."

"Forever, Mia. Until the very end of time."

Their lips met then in a tender, passionate kiss.

THE EDITOR'S CORNER

Bantam Books has a *very* special treat for you next month—Nora Roberts's most ambitious, most sizzling novel yet . . .

SWEET REVENGE

Heroine Adrianne, the daughter of a fabled Hollywood beauty and an equally fabled Arab playboy, leads a remarkable double life. The paparazzi and the gossip columnists know her as a modern princess, a frivolous socialite flitting from exclusive watering spot to glittering charity ball. No one knows her as The Shadow, the most extraordinary jewel thief of the decade. She hones her skills at larceny as she parties with the superrich, stealing their trinkets and baubles just for practice . . . for she has a secret plan for the ultimate heist—a spectacular plan to even a bitter score. Her secret is her own until Philip Chamberlain enters her life. Once a renowned thief himself, he's now one of Interpol's smartest, toughest cops . . . and he's falling wildly in love with Adrianne!

SWEET REVENGE will be on sale during the beginning of December when your LOVESWEPTs come into the stores. Be sure to ask your bookseller right now to reserve a copy especially for you.

Now to the delectable LOVESWEPTs you can count on to add to your holiday fun . . . and excitement.

Our first love story next month carries a wonderful round number—LOVESWEPT #300! **LONG TIME COMING,** by Sandra Brown, is as thrilling and original as any romance Sandra has ever written. Law Kincaid, the heart-stoppingly handsome astronaut hero, is in a towering rage when he comes storming up Marnie Hibbs's front walk. He thinks she has been sending him blackmail letters claiming he has a teenage son. As aghast as she is, and still wildly attracted to Law, whom she met seventeen years before when she was just a teen, Marnie tries to put him off and hold her secret close. But the golden and glorious man is determined to wrest the truth from her at any cost! A beautiful love story!

(continued)

Welcome back Peggy Webb, author of LOVESWEPT #301, **HALLIE'S DESTINY**, a marvelous love story featuring a gorgeous "gypsy" whom you met in previous books, Hallie Donovan. A rodeo queen with a heart as big as Texas, Hallie was the woman Josh Butler wanted—he knew it the second he set eyes on her! Josh was well aware of the havoc a bewitching woman like Hallie could wreak in a man's life, but he couldn't resist her. When Josh raked her with his sexy golden eyes and took her captive on a carpet of flowers, Hallie felt a miraculous joy . . . and a great fear, for Josh couldn't—wouldn't—share his life and its problems with her. He sets limits on their love that drive Hallie away . . . until neither can endure without the other. A thrilling romance!

New author Gail Douglas scores another winner with **FLIRTING WITH DANGER**, LOVESWEPT #302. Cassie Walters is a spunky and gorgeous lady who falls under the spell of Bret Parker, a self-made man who is as rich as he is sexy . . . and utterly relentless when it comes to pursuing Cassie. Bret's not quite the womanizer the press made him out to be, as Cassie quickly learns. (I think you'll relish as much as I did the scene in which Michael and Cassie see each other for the first time. Never has an author done more for baby powder and diapers than Gail does in that encounter!) Cassie is terrified of putting down roots . . . and Bret is quite a family man. He has to prove to the woman with whom he's fallen crazily in love that she is brave enough to share his life. A real charmer of a love story crackling with excitement!

In **MANHUNT**, LOVESWEPT #303, Janet Evanovich has created two delightfully adorable and lusty protagonists in a setting that is fascinating. Alexandra Scott—fed up with her yuppie life-style and yearning for a husband and family—has chucked it all and moved to the Alaskan wilderness. She hasn't chosen her new home in a casual way; she's done it using statistics—in Alaska men outnumber women four to one. And right off the bat she meets a man who's one in a million, a dizzyingly attractive avowed bachelor, Michael Casey. But Alex can't be rational about Michael; she loses her head, right along with her heart to him. And to capture him she has to be shameless in her seduction. . . . A true delight!

Get ready to be transported into the heart of a small Southern town and have your funny bone tickled while your
(continued)

heart is warmed when you read **RUMOR HAS IT,** LOVE-SWEPT #304, by Tami Hoag. The outrageous gossip that spreads about Nick Leone when he comes to town to open a restaurant has Katie Quaid as curious as every other woman in the vicinity. She's known as an ice princess, but the moment she and Nick get together she's melting for him. You may shed a tear for Katie—she's had unbearable tragedy in her young life—and you'll certainly gasp with her when Nick presents her with a shocking surprise. A wonderfully fresh and emotionally moving love story!

That marvelous Nick Capoletti you met in Joan Elliott Pickart's last two romances gets his own true love in **SERENITY COVE,** LOVESWEPT #305. When Pippa Pauling discovered Nick Capoletti asleep on the floor of the cabin he'd rented in her cozy mountain lake resort, she felt light-headed with longing and tempted beyond resistance. From the second they first touched, Nick knew Pippa was hearth and home and everything he wanted in life. But Pippa feared that the magic they wove was fleeting. No one could fall in love so fast and make it real for a lifetime. But leave it to Capoletti! In a thrilling climax that takes Pippa and Nick back to Miracles Casino in Las Vegas and the gang there, Pippa learns she can indeed find forever in Nick's arms. A scorching and touching romance from our own Joan Elliott Pickart!

Also in Bantam's general list next month is a marvelous mainstream book that features love, murder, and shocking secrets—**MIDNIGHT SINS,** by new author Ellin Hall. This is a fast-paced and thrilling book with an unforgettable heroine. Don't miss it.

Have a wonderful holiday season.

Carolyn Nichols

Carolyn Nichols
Editor
LOVESWEPT
Bantam Books
666 Fifth Avenue
New York, NY 10103